MW01172886

TO LOVE AND DIE IN ATLANTA

VOL. 1

SA'ID SALAAM

URBAN AESOP PUBLICATIONS

Email: saidmasalaam@gmail.com

Cover Designer: Adriane Hall

Proofreader: KaiCee White

DEDICATION

In loving memory of Blair (Amin) Singleton
From Allah we come, to Allah we return. Ameen.

CHAPTER 1

"*Y*ou finished packing Marquis?" Marquita Williams asked her handsome young son. At sixteen he looked exactly like his daddy did at sixteen when he made her a sixteen year old mother. The same smooth, black skin. Same white smile that put that same dimple on display.

The young girls around their southwest Atlanta neighborhood were already chasing him around just like she once chased his daddy. The police chased the young criminal as well and caught him before she gave birth to their baby boy. His son would be just shy of twenty when or if he made it home from his twenty year bid.

"I **been** finished packing!" he happily cheered. Most teens hate having to move but Marquis wasn't them. His rough neighborhood was infested with the Roller gang. He was being pressured to join the gang every day he stepped from his house. The two sport **star** would give them bragging rights over their rival Riders gang since he was headed for the NFL, NBA or both if he wanted.

"I know you hate leaving your friends behind?" Marquita had to ask, since she wasn't quite sure.

1

He only had one friend that she knew of for sure. A teammate called Mayhem for his antics on and off the basketball court. He had enough talent to at least get a full ride to any division one college but a severe addiction to the streets was definitely going to hold him back, if not kill or incarcerate him. He long ago gave in to the gang affiliation and was leader in the Rollers.

"Nah," he quickly responded, causing his pretty mother to twist her lips and cock her head in a dare.

"Not even Bomb-quisha?" she challenged and put a little more twist in her lips. She had recently caught him digging her out real good when she came home early from work. Then, almost made him pull out so she could confirm he was wearing the protection she persistently pushed on him. Young girls now read scouting reports and will put a baby on an upcoming millionaire.

"She'll be a'ight," he assured. He was sure too because Bomb-quisha was a hoe, and hoes gonna be a'ight no matter what. Open legs and open mouths have opened doors before doors were even invented. Marquis was looking forward to seeing what these bougie girls in his new suburban school were talking about.

"I know she is!" his mother huffed sarcastically since she knew the girl was a hoe as well. She had grown up around enough hoes in the hood to know one when she saw one. Not to mention she grew up with Bomb-quisha's mother, who was also a hoe. She came from a long line of hoes dating back to her Navajo ancestors.

"What about Leon?" Marquis asked of her on again off again boyfriend. A lot of which depended upon whether she was on or off her period since he only served one purpose in her life. He could have been a plumber since he laid pipe on demand, but he would have to leave his mama's basement for that.

"What about him?" Marquita shot back and rolled her eyes and neck like she learned from her mama.

"So, he's not gonna be coming to the new house?" he dared just she just did him. He could do better than his hood rat but wondered if his mother wanted to. Judging by the thumping on the wall whenever the man slept over she was pretty fond of the pretty boy.

"He good right there at his mama house!" she replied quickly. What she didn't say was she was looking forward to seeing what those sophisticated men at her new job were talking about. Life had taken a turn from bleak to bright when Marquis was named one of the top point guards in the nation.

Now she was offered a new job and house for him to transfer to a wealthy suburban enclave north of the city. Leon was content to sell dime bags of mediocre weed to finance his Jordan collection and latest game system. She wanted more from life while he was content running in place on the treadmill of life, going nowhere fast.

"I'm finna run over there and say goodbye to Miss Mary," Marquita managed while her lady parts tingled at the thought of Miss Mary's son. Mary and Leon were as close in age as she and her son but she didn't hang out in the same clubs like Mary did.

"Mmhm, tell Leon I said hey," Marquis quipped knowingly and picked up the remote.

"Watch yo mouth 'lil boy," she fussed on her way out to do just that. Half a smile twisted a corner of her mouth upward at the sight of her old sedan. It had served her well but she saw a new car in her future. With a new house and new job it was only right that she bought a new car. Even if her section eight was augmented by the school and donors in exchange for the state championship her son was sure to bring them.

"I shole ain't finna miss this mess!" Marquita fussed as she stepped out into the muggy night air. It was still in the upper eighties but the weed and gun smoke seemed to make the hood that much hotter. She had been by the new house and knew her old lingo would be better left behind. She lifted her chin like a lady she saw coming out of one of the houses and tried again. "I won't miss this place one bit."

"Hey girl!" a tiny woman called 'Lil Bit' called out. She was already of a small stature but a lifelong crack habit had only left a lil bit left. The large head on the tiny body made her look like she had been drawn by a kindergartner.

"Ion got no spare change chile!" Marquita shot back to shut down the request she knew was coming. The junkie was used to rejection so she shrugged it off and kept moving.

"Finna find a spare dick to suck," she huffed and stepped out onto Cascade to hail passing cars. It wouldn't be long before someone happened along who didn't mind playing Russian roulette with his life. Sticking a bare dick inside of street walkers was a lot more dangerous than a revolver with a live round in one of the chambers.

"Last time..." Marquita told herself as she made her way up the rickety steps to the front porch. It was just one of many repairs a real man would have made if one lived there. Leon was just a male and only stayed there. There is a difference.

"Come on in chile!" Miss Mary cheered happily when she looked to see who was creeping up the stairs and saw her favorite from the many women her son entertained. She had hoped her son would have married this woman but it was just one of so many other unfulfilled hopes she had for her son.

"Hey Miss Mary!" Marquita cheered back and hugged her neck. She declined the glass of malt liquor she extended and sat. "You know we finna move."

"You taking Leon with you?" the woman asked probably the way a pack mule that was tired of carrying shit would ask if it could talk.

"Hell naw!" she shot back before she could filter it.

"I know that's right," his mother sighed and shook her head.

They both shared a good laugh but only Marquita knew it would be their last laugh. This would be her last visit. She would leave the hood in the rear view mirror of her life for life.

"What y'all laughing at?" Leon asked as he emerged from his basement lair. The timing just made the two women laugh that much harder. He had no idea he was the butt of this joke and cracked that million dollar smile that made him a baby daddy ten times over.

"Nothing boy," his mama said as she whined down. "You helping them move tomorrow?"

"Huh?" Leon asked immediately. Not because he didn't hear but needed another second to formulate an excuse. "I'ma try. Woody 'sposed to come by and, we finna, they 'sposed to be hiring..."

"Oh yeah. OK," Marquita cut in to cut off his feeble excuses before they disgusted her to the point of abandoning what she came for. She had already rented a truck and hired some men from the same day labor place Leon works for when he feels like working.

"Come on down," he invited like the partially finished basement was his own pad. It had been when he moved down at sixteen but twenty years later it was just sad. It did have a king bed, hundred inch TV and PS-5 which was all he needed in life.

"See ya," Marquita said over her shoulder but left off 'soon' or 'later' since she didn't mean it. It really was goodbye since she was done with the hood as soon as the sun rose on tomorrow. Which is the good thing about the sun, it always rises to shine light on another chance.

"OK baby," the woman said and went back to her warm beer and cheesy sitcoms.

"Do I need to call the fire truck?" Marquita winced as they descended into the smoke filled basement.

"For what?" Leon asked and scrunched his handsome face into a ball of smooth, brown confusion.

"Good thing you're pretty," she laughed and got another 'huh' out of him. She plopped down on the bed and crossed her big, brown legs for attention. That he got.

"Fine ass!" Leon said and sat down beside her like that spider.

"Mmhm..." she hummed as he gripped that big brown leg and leaned in to kiss her neck. Her legs spread along with his kisses until his tongue was down her throat and fingers plunging in and out of her soaked vagina.

Somehow a titty found its way out and ended up in his mouth. She scrambled to get his claim to fame out of his pants and tugged it with both hands. They both stripped out of their clothes between kisses and gropes and made their way to the middle of the bed.

"Bruh..." Marquita chided when he attempted to line his rock hard dick up between her slippery swollen lips.

"Oh yeah!" he laughed and popped himself on the head like he could have had a V8.

"Mmhm," she hummed and twisted her other lips up since she knew better. He would have gladly run up in her raw just like all the other neighborhood hoes let him. She didn't though so he reached for his supply of extra large condoms.

Marquita couldn't help not to shake her head at the waste of the big dick, chiseled body and handsome face. She could only hope the bougie men of her new life came fully equipped like this. Leon stole her from her thoughts when he rubbed the latex wrapped dick against her labia. She shared the kiss he offered as he began to ease inside.

"Wait!" she shouted so abruptly he looked over to the stairs to make sure his mama wasn't coming. After all, the washer and dryer was a few feet away. But that wasn't the case tonight as she flipped him over onto his back.

"Oh, you wanna ride this horse huh!" he bragged, even though he shouldn't have at the moment. He may have been well hung but was hit or miss on how he slung that thang. Some nights he was Sammy Sosa in the pussy and knocked it clean out the park. Other nights he was gone in sixty seconds, or less. He blamed it on the good pussy but that didn't help her much.

"Mmhm. And, I'ma need you..." she said as she worked him inside of her. "Be quiet..."

Leon didn't like to be told what to do but he did like the stroke she developed. He compensated by leaning up and sucking one of the big, brown nipples in front of him. He could only grip her hips and hold on as she rocked and rolled like a rock band.

"Grrrr..." Marquita growled as electric currents began tingling her toes. This was going to be a good one so she adjusted her grip on the dollar store sheets and switched gears.

Leon inched closer to climax with each thrust, drag and grind of her hips. He almost called out but remembered her instructions. All he could do was cover his mouth with his hand and grunt. Marquita was a pretty chick but her face transformed into a pretty demon mask when she came.

"Fuck!" she howled with her head towards the ceiling. Her tight box convulsed and contracted around his thick dick and kicked him over the precipice he had so precariously teetered upon. He came as hard as she and gave the latex all it could handle.

They kissed vigorously as they writhed in the mutual pleasure of mutual climax. If they could live their lives in such synchronicity they could take over the world. They couldn't, wouldn't though because he sold weed from his mother's basement and she was moving on to a better life. This nut was a good nut, but it was only a nut. Not an ordinary nut either, it was the last nut.

"I need to go," Marquita moaned without moving, now that she had what she came for.

"Want me to walk you?" he asked, but didn't move. Marquita

pressed her lips together to keep the slick remark from escaping. The fact that he had to even ask was all the reasons she was leaving him behind.

"You better walk that chile home!" Miss Mary shouted from above their head and stomped her foot since she heard the episode come to a crescendo. Voices easily traveled from floor to floor since he didn't repair the worn out floor boards.

"Nosey ass," Leon whispered so she wouldn't hear and rolled off the bed. His life was pretty simple since his biggest dilemma was which pair of knockoff Jordans to wear. He settled on the patent leather joints and joined her getting dressed. Watching a woman shimmy into her panties is a favorite pastime of many men. Leon was one of them and paused to watch until the show ended.

Marquita let out a sigh as Leon let her out the rear door for the last time. He led her around front and up the block. Holding hands would have been nice but Leon didn't have it in him. Instead he babbled about the bull shit bubbling about the hood. Who fucked or shot whom, while her eyes took a final tour.

"I want an ice cream," she decided when the corner store came into view. The sight of a little girl skipping out, licking a soft serve cone meant a few things. One her parents weren't shit for her to be out this late on her own. And two, the ice cream machine was working.

"I got you!" Leon offered to her surprise.

"For real!" she reeled at the second rarity of the night. The machine working and him paying was too much good luck to ignore so she decided to play the lottery as well.

"Hell yeah!" Leon cheered and produced a large roll of cash to prove it. Heads turned as the whiff of cash filled the air. The crack-stitutes changed directions to see if they could suck a few bucks out of the man. The jack boys also smelled the money and converged from three different directions. It was common for them to fight and shoot each other over the right to rob a victim. Sorta like wild animals fighting over a carcass in the Serengeti.

"Watch out..." Marquita was saying as two feral youths crossed the street in a hurry. They wanted to catch him before he got into the store to spend some of their money. The malice in their eyes gave an eerie glint in the yellow street lights.

"I see them..." Leon replied through clenched teeth as he slid a hand into his pocket where a slightly used 380 hung out for fuck shit like this. The young thugs stopped abruptly and spun on their heels to walk the other way. "Thought so!"

"Le..." Marquita tried to call when she turned to see what spooked the teens. He may have thought the peashooter in his pocket did it but a lone gunman raised his gun. Her mouth opened as wide as her eyes but words wouldn't come. Not that he would have heard them over the roar of the huge revolver.

The man fired a round through one side of Leon's thick skull and out the other. Marquita felt the warm spray of blood and brains splash her face, along with the sting of bone fragments the large slug sent her way. The man had what he came for and turned away.

Marquita was frozen in place from fear and shock. The shock of seeing a man murdered paled only in comparison to the rush of people who rushed to collect the bills that fell from his dead hands. They scrambled for the money like kids to candy from a freshly cracked piñata. Even that shock wasn't shit to the one that came as the human vultures began digging through his pockets. Some small kids pulled his Jordans from his feet and ran off.

Shocking yes, but just another night in the city of Atlanta.

CHAPTER 2

"*Mama*. Mama..." Marquis called for a fifth time, louder yet still softly. This time was loud enough to steal her attention from the brutal murder that was stuck on repeat in her mind. She wasn't able to tell the police what she saw since the hood had rules against snitching. Couldn't sleep either since the vivid violence kept replaying on her eyelids.

"Huh?" Marquita asked as even her title of mama confused her. She cast a confused look around at the boxes piled high and strained to figure out why.

"The um, truck finna be here in a few," he reminded.

"Oh yeah. We finna move," she recalled and stood. "We out this hoe!"

"Mama, you still gotta bathe tho," he reminded softly.

"You tryna say I stink?" she asked playfully.

"Nah, you just got..." Marquis said and pointed at his own face as a reminder of the mess on her own face. She reached up and touched the traces of the homicide she happened to be standing too close to. The blood had dried an eerie black like an abstract

"Oh yeah," she sighed and went to wash the blood and brains from her face just as the store owner sprayed the sidewalk in front of his establishment.

The hot water worked wonders and sent the shock and blood stains swirling down the drain. She, like so many hood dwellers had seen so many acts of violence she was nearly numb to it. By the time she was dry and dressed her focus was on the new house. Hearing the movers arrive put a new pep in her step as she stepped out to give directions.

"Y'all don't break my shit now!" she huffed and directed traffic until the truck was loaded. The fully loaded truck wouldn't halfway fill the new house so she planned to do some shopping once she started the new job.

"Dang," Marquis said in semi shock when they looked around the empty unit one last time. He recalled moving in nearly a lifetime ago, and now they were moving out.

"I know right," his mother cosigned but refused to look back. When moving on, one should never look back. She led the way to her old beater that was fully loaded with boxes and bags. The raggedy car was next to go since she started a new job on Monday.

The mother and son stared straight ahead and barely breathed as they left the hood. Both were determined to never return once they made it out. They had both seen the hood swallow whole souls. Generations of families stuck in the vicious cycle of poverty and violence.

Marquita's eye dipped to the spot where Leon lost his life a few hours ago. Not a trace of the violence remained before his body got cold. Kids played and skipped where blood and brains recently littered the sidewalk. Her eyes shifted back and her head lifted. They were almost out, nothing would stop them.

"Marquis! Marquis!" Bomb-quisha called from the sidewalk when she saw the car passing.

"Don't stop mama!" Marquis demanded, looking straight

ahead. Marquita began to turn but her son shut it down. "Un-uh! Don't even look!"

"Just trifling!" she laughed as the girl shouted his name. Marquita saw her future of chasing cars when she ran into the street, flailing her hands.

"Mmhm," he hummed in agreement as if he hadn't rocked her one last time last night. He didn't even tell her they were moving. Nor most of his friends for that matter, but they would figure it out.

A few more turns and they pulled onto the highway. And just like that the hood was behind them.

"SUP MAMA. Me and Keto finna hi the ma," Carey slurred to his mother. The woman winced as she attempted to complete the words he clipped.

"Hit the mall?" she deciphered but had a better question for the future valedictorian. "Why are you speaking like that?"

"Same reason he dresses like that," Carey senior surmised. He had worked his ass off to move his family from a comfortable middle class existence to this exclusive subdivision. It was nestled on the edge of the upper echelon areas he was headed.

They were just a few of the colored sprinkles on the otherwise vanilla cone of this subdivision. All eyes were always on the few black families so image was everything. He worked at the right financial firm, wore the right suites and drove the right electric vehicle.

His wife was light enough to compensate for his dark skin and carried herself like she had been here her whole life. She hadn't though since she came from a Virginia tobacco farm before meeting Carey Rollins in college. Image was everything and everything about the Rollins was right except their only son's preoccupation with all things hood.

"Err body dresses like this shawty!" he proclaimed and lifted his arms to show his skinny pants and unisex shirt. It was really a blouse until these suspect rappers started wearing them. The line between hetero and homo blurred by the day.

"Not 'err one lives in a half million dollar house, drives sixty thousand dollar cars and has two loving parents!" Mr Rollins snapped. He didn't scrape, scrap and claw his way out of the hood to raise a hood rat in his own home.

"Not everyone has scholarship offers from several schools in scholastics and basketball either!" Mrs Rollins defended. She didn't like her son playing make believe bad guy any more than her husband but at the end of the day it was just make believe. Carey was a good kid, going through yet another phase in his life. The garage was filled with the equipment and remnants of plenty of the other phases he had gone through.

"Tell him mama!" Carey junior chided. He always liked when his mother came to his aid against his father. The two parents had totally opposite approaches to parenting. Mr was determined to hold him accountable while his Mrs insisted upon free passes through life.

Why wouldn't she when she was riding well off the free pass of being married to the hardworking husband. He was a goal digger while she was a gold digger. She kept a clean house courtesy of the mobile maid service and ordered boxed food kits to feed them. A careful ration of sex helped keep the reigns on the relationship. The day before allowance was good for some sex, while special request could get his dick sucked.

"You know what..." Mr Rollins asked but that was the answer as well since he walked off. There was always plenty of work to do to drag the dead weight along to the next stage in life. Changing zip codes cost money so he retreated to his office to make some.

"Mind if I use your car mother?" Carey asked. He knew to turn his hood persona on and off like a light switch.

"And what's wrong with your Audi?" she asked since she loved to name drop. A purse was never just a purse. It was Hermes or Birkin. Her walk-in closet was actually a spare bedroom with a walk-in closet. Filled with Gucci, Fendi and other reminders that she had come a long way from that tobacco farm.

"Nothing. Your Mercedes is just cooler!" he cheered, smiled and won her over just like he did the girls in his school. The handsome senior was also the star point guard, for now since the coach just recruited Marquis.

"Let me get my Coach," she sighed and relented. They laughed and smiled just as the U-haul truck rumbled into their world. It alone was a bad sign since folks around here used more prestigious movers and didn't haul anything themselves.

"What is a U-haul mother?" Carey asked as he and Marquis locked eyes in passing.

"A bad sign..." she replied as she locked in on Marquita behind the wheel of the beat down beater she drove. It seemed to sense it had an audience and blew a puff of smoke from the exhaust to say hello.

"You see these rich folks just staring?" Marquis asked as they pulled into the new driveway to their new home.

"Be nice. They will probably want to come help?" she replied and waved. The wave seemed to startle the mother and son from their gawking. He hopped into the vehicle and pulled away. She dipped inside to keep watch from her window like the other neighbors were doing. "Or not..."

"Least we got these guys," Marquis said as the three moving men piled out of the truck's bench seat.

"Yeah..." Marquita agreed and shot a glance back over to where Mrs Rollins once was. She didn't see her since she was now peering through the blinds.

"What kind of hoochie mama, section eight mess is this?"

Mrs Rollins wondered scornfully as when she noticed the tiny shorts Marquita was dressed down in since she was working.

"What's that Sinclair?" her husband asked as he came in behind her.

"The new neighbors..." she repeated and wondered which one of the moving men was her husband since all the women in the de sac had husbands. An unmarried woman would just be scandalous.

"Oh OK. I'm headed..." Carey was saying but it didn't matter since she wasn't listening. Instead she went back to investigating the new neighbors.

"MY BOY C-NOTE pulling up in da Benzo!" Kenneth announced when Carey arrived to pick him up. He had instantly transformed into Keto when he saw him. His mother had the same model Benz but not the same trust in her son. He had his own new Mercedes courtesy of his absentee father, so he would not be driving hers.

"Sup homie," Carey asked his homeboy while looking for his homeboy's sister. Kenneth had a twin sister with a fat ass and penchant for bad boys. Most of the girls in school did but the school didn't have any. That's why Kenneth and Carey decided to become some.

"She's not here," Keto huffed when he saw his friend looking towards the house,

"Who?" Carey asked innocently.

"Kelondra. She went to the mall with Katie," he replied and slid into the passenger seat.

"Anyway, you got that?" he asked and looked over as his friend pulled the gun from his waistband. "Sweet!"

"I know right!" Kenneth cheered as they fondled his mother's pistol.

"Well let's hit the trap and go get this guap!" Carey said and backed out. Ironically he headed down to the same hood Marquis and Marquita just escaped from. He had a mid level weed connection that allowed him to sell to his customers at school.

Carey didn't sell drugs for the money even though he made plenty of it. His father was wealthy enough to provide every-thing his family needed. It was the wants he couldn't supply. Both mother and son were clout chasers and that cost more than he made.

"Game time," Keto announced when they reached the raggedy apartments where their connect lived.

"Let me get that..." C-note said and extended his empty palm. It held the pistol when he pulled it back. Carey wanted the gun for several reasons, none of them good.

For one he knew his friend wouldn't bust a grape in a food fight. Even though food was the only type of fight either had been in. Second, Carey was looking forward to busting his gun just like the rappers rapped in every song on every station, every other minute. No wonder these kids minds are filled with malice and murder, sex, drugs and violence.

"Come on!" a voice hollered back from the inside of the door. C-note turned the knob to open the door.

"Dang!" Keto grimaced when a wave of smoke swept over them as they entered.

"Smoking good ain't you!" C-note laughed and inhaled deeply.

"Hell yeah," Man-man laughed from the sofa. He was so high he couldn't even lean forward so he pointed to the pounds of weed on the table. "That's you."

"And this you," C-note nodded towards Keto who produced the stack of cash.

"Twenty bands," Keto proudly announced.

"Just put it on the table shawty," Man-man drawled. He had

overcharged these nerdy kids so much he wasn't worried about any short money. He could only get a thousand dollars a pound in the hood but they cost ten times as much in the suburbs. C-note and Keto would turn around and sell the same weed for fifty dollars a gram and make plenty of money. Even with what they smoked they stood to double what they spent.

"A'ight then shawty," Keto repeated, causing C-note to groan. His friend never could quite nail that particular slang word.

"We'll be back in a 'frew days," C-note said like they say around there.

"Yeah, a'ight," Man-man laughed and flicked the remote.

"We need to rob they ass!" Scooter declared when he came from the back. It was his job to standby with the chopper during sales. His assignment was to come out blasting in the case of some fuck shit.

"For what? They giving they bread voluntarily!" he laughed. It wasn't broken so there was no need to fix it.

CHAPTER 3

"*J*'m out," C-note announced on his way to the front door. His father just shook his head at the slang while his wife patted his hand.

"Be safe," she called after him as the door closed behind him. Once she got a chance she planned to fuss him out about the weed smell left behind in her car.

"Speaking of safe..." Carey senior said suggestively and wiggled his eyebrows.

"Is that all you think of?" his wife fussed. She once heard some relationship guru advise women to ration the pussy to their husbands. Reason being scarcity adds value but it doesn't make much sense. Not when side chicks and escorts were dishing it out like the buffet. Chicks slinging pussy like white folks sling frisbees in the park and this nigga telling them to ration it.

"Actually, no. I mainly think about the mortgage. Bills, groceries, college, retirement..." he rambled on. "So, every now and then I would like a little sex."

"See!" she insisted like an 'ah-hah' moment. She didn't have a rebuttal but didn't need one since she was a drama queen. She hopped to her feet and stormed off. "I just can't with you!"

"Evidently I can't with you either," he sighed and shook his head. There was only one thing left to do so he retreated to his office to do it. His favorite porn sites were bookmarked for easy access. As was the lube in a side draw. His son was out on a date with Kelondra, while he had a date with his hand.

Carey junior bent a few corners in his Audi until he reached Keto's house. He had picked him up earlier for their run into the city but this time he came for his sister. Their mother opened the door looking young enough to be an older sister.

"Well hello there Carey," she greeted happily. She genuinely liked the upstanding kid from the good family and hoped he would be a good influence on her son who had adopted a hood persona as of late. Carey knew to speak properly around her which was why she didn't mind him dating her daughter.

"Good evening Mrs Worthington," he offered politely and smiled.

"Mizz," she reminded since the divorce was final a few weeks ago. She intended to keep the surname she shared with her children but just added the miz.

"Hey Carey!" Kelondra sang and smiled as she came down the stairs in a tasteful dress that reached below her knees.

"Hello. You look great," he replied as her mother nodded approvingly at her attire. Her son was the only one dressing like some inner city hoodlum.

"You guys have fun! Until twelve," the mother announced and reminded them both of her curfew. There was plenty of trouble to be had before midnight but rules were rules.

"OK!" they replied on the way out to the car. Mizz Worthington smiled in approval when she watched Carey open the passenger door and hold open for her daughter to be seated like a perfect gentleman.

"Thanks," Kelondra replied when he came around to the

driver's seat. As soon as they pulled away she pulled the dress over her head and tossed it in the back seat. Kelondra was still in the dress because this was Ki-ki seated beside him. She had an alter ego outside of the house as well.

"Damn shawty!" C-note exclaimed now that he could get back into character. He looked down at the firm thighs against his leather seats. They were as nice as the ass cleavage hanging out the bottom of the Daisy Duke shorts she wore under the dress. A halter top strained to contain the big young breast she took everywhere she went.

"Where the weed at my nigga!" she cheered and flipped her hair. A healthy crop of hair was past her shoulders and bone straight from a fresh trip to the stylist. Still she wished she could wear wigs and weaves like her favorite celebrity hoochie mamas wore. There was no way of keeping her mother from seeing that so she had to settle for her own hair.

"Hmp shawty," he grunted and passed her a weed pipe packed with his personal supply. He had plenty left to sell at the party they were headed to. Her brother was already there handling sales as well. They would sell out before school on Monday.

Kelondra put a flame to the pipe and inhaled. After a coughing fit she lit the lighter again and held it so C-note could take a pull. They did that back and forth until they reached the swank subdivision where the party was being held. A class-mate's parents were liberal enough to allow him to throw weekly parties.

"Sup y'all!" Keto smiled when his sister and best friend arrived. The wide smile was twofold since sales were good plus he was good and high.

"Hey guys!" Katie cheesed and wobbled under his arm. The pretty white girl's face was pretty pink from all the weed and alcohol she was consuming.

"Sup," C-note replied as the two girls huddled up to giggle and gossip.

"I sold the fuck out is what's up!" he replied and came out with a fistful of cash.

"Shit shawty I'm 'posed to meet David, Dino, Sarah..." C-note said and read a list of some of their best customers. They had already recouped their initial investment just like their fathers did in the business world.

"Well, handle your business. I'm about to handle mine," Keto said and scurried Katie away to one of the empty bedrooms. She and Kelondra were best of friends but held different views about their vaginas.

Kelondra was a tight lipped virgin which kept her lips tight. She wasn't necessarily saving it for marriage but wasn't giving it up just yet. She and Carey had been dating for a few months but she hadn't put out to him. There were other ways to keep one's boyfriend happy and hymen intact.

Now Katie on the other hand was a hoe. A hoe's hoe who put the O in hoe. She was running through the varsity teams like omicron. Definitely the proverbial doorknob and it was now Keto's turn. They had to wait for one of the rooms to become empty since there was traditionally a lot of screwing going on at the parties.

"Hey you," C-note greeted when he finished making his rounds. All the weed he brought had been exchanged for cash and he was ready to go. First he had to wait for Ki-ki to finish twerking with her classmates. The bougie suburban kids mimicked most of what went on in most hood parties and clubs. Except they weren't going to kill each other. That's not to say one of these white kids wouldn't shoot up the school one day, but the party was safe.

"Hey yourself..." Kelondra giggled as he pulled her towards the gate. It was eleven thirty which gave them a few minutes of alone time before her curfew. Both knew exactly how they were going to spend it.

Kelondra hit the weed again once Carey pulled from the curb. After getting a few pulls she passed and held it up to his mouth while he drove. He returned the favor by reaching between her legs to rub her crotch.

"Sssss," she hissed and soaked her panties. The shorts were too tight to pull aside so she undid the buttons to allow access. Limited access, that is," Don't sssss, put it inside."

"I won't," he vowed even though he would if she hadn't stopped him. He had to content himself with the slippery outer lips as he drove. It may not have been enough for him but was plenty for her.

"Mmmm, mmmm, mmhm," she whimpered and moaned as an orgasm crept up her spine. Her body bucked involuntarily when she bust a nut all over his fingers. She had regained her composure by the time he pulled onto her cul de sac. "Guess I need to return the flavor?"

"Or we could climb in the backseat and..." he suggested.

"Or, I could just go inside?" she asked and reached for the door handle.

"Come here," Carey laughed and pulled her across to him. She leaned up and in for a kiss. Their tongues twirled around in each other's mouths until he pulled her hand down to his erection.

Kelondra unzipped his zipper and scrambled to release his dick. It was so hard she had trouble getting it out the hole in his skinny jeans. Just another reason not to wear them because sometimes you need to get your dick out quickly. This was one of those times since the curfew clock was ticking.

"Here..." he said and slid the seat back. Carey lifted up enough to unbutton his pants and free his erection. A second later it was engulfed in the warm, wonderful heat of her mouth. "Fuck!"

"Mmhm," Kelondra hummed and went back to her training. Hanging with hoes has its advantages and disadvantages. Katie teaching her how to properly suck a dick was definitely on the plus side. She had taught her a medley of techniques but the 'tip and tug' worked best with time constraints. She took the tip in her mouth and tugged on the shaft until his legs began to shift beneath him. Katie warned her about that and she was able to escape seconds before he exploded.

"Fuck! Fuck" Carey exclaimed twice. Once for the good nut and again when it landed on his steering wheel, windshield and pants.

"I bet," Kelondra giggled proudly and pulled the door open. She had one foot on her driveway when he pulled her back. "I gotta go inside!"

"I know but uh..." he reminded by looking at her thick thighs.

"Oh yeah!" she laughed and retrieved her dress from the backseat. She pulled it over her head and popped a kiss on his cheek before rushing inside to beat the clock.

CHAPTER 4

"*D*ang!" Marquis exclaimed when he met his mother in the kitchen. It was the first morning in the new house and they could already hear the difference.

"I know right!" she laughed. The hood is usually still early on a Sunday morning since most of the creeps who come out at night creep back in before the sun rises.

Life was already bustling in the suburbs since they didn't hang out all night around there. A few lawnmowers were already in motion on the manicured lawns. Homeowners take pride in their curb appeal and that took work. Work needed to be done before the hot sun began beating down.

"Un-uh, we gotta get some blinds!" Marquita announced when she saw a passing car peering into the open windows.

"We need a lot of stuff," he sighed. It wasn't a complaint since he was grateful for the new house. It was his multi-sport prowess that made it happen but he was still grateful.

"And we finna, I mean, we gone get it," she corrected even if it wasn't completely correct. Another car with another gawker drove slowly by so she decided on a quick fix. "Grab that newspaper we used to pack the dishes. This will have to do 'til we hit the Walmart..."

The passing cars weren't the only ones interested in the new neighbors. One neighbor across the street had taken a particular interest in who would be living in an eye shot.

"I know she is not..." Sinclair huffed.

"What's wrong dear?" Carey senior asked as he came up behind her.

"The new neighbor is putting newspapers in her windows!" she fussed and spun on her feet. She rushed over to the kitchen drawer to find the home owners association charter.

"Maybe we can welcome them to the neighborhood? A cake perhaps? Cookies..." he asked as she dug.

"Ah-ha!" she proudly proclaimed when she produced the papers. Now she had to peruse the paragraphs for the particular print she needed. It's discovery warranted another, 'Ah-ha' and she was out the door.

"Sinclair..." her husband called after her. He was relieved to see the new neighbors drive by as they came out of the house.

"I think that lady wants you?" Marquis wondered when he saw Mrs Rollins running across her lawn waving the documents.

"I'll see them when we get back. I ain't tryna meet nobody looking a mess," his mother declared and took a peek in the rearview as she patted her weave.

Marquis just shrugged and took in the new neighborhood that was now his home. They had corners out here too but no corner store. No corner store meant no dope boys standing out front. Which translated into no robberies or shoot outs.

"Ain't seen 'nare junkie since we left the Bluff!" Marquita offered like a mind reader. Of course there were plenty of junkies out in the suburbs too. They just dressed nicer and used different drugs.

"And when I go pro I'ma buy you your own house!

Anywhere you want!" he insisted. Going pro was a given along with the millions that came along with it. He had a fleet of cars and jewelry mapped out in his mind but buying his mother a car was atop his list.

"I know you are baby," she cheesed and continued on to the mall. The old beater was smoking like a peace pipe when they arrived. She parked as far away from the entrance as possible since she was just as embarrassed by the old car as her son. He nodded his approval and appreciation as they walked over to the entrance.

"These bougie folks shole be some lookie-loos!" he complained as all eyes were on either him or his mama. She seemed to get as much attention from the women as she did from the men.

"Ion know what they looking at," she said as her round ass jiggled and jumped around in the loose fitting sweat pants she wore. That kind of fine simply can not be subdued. That and the blue weave in her head.

Marquis got his fair share of attention since his was a new face in a sea of familiar ones. The mall was the place to see and be seen and stayed packed. Most of the kids his age attended his new school but he had yet to start classes.

"Hubba, hubba!" Katie announced lustfully and licked her lips as she looked the luscious lad from head to toe. Like she hadn't just gotten fucked by her friend's brother a few hours ago.

"He is cute," Kelondra agreed, slightly subdued since she just sucked some dick around that same time. Kenneth's curfew was an hour later even though they were the same age. Men and women are not the same and their mother wanted them to understand it at an early age.

"He's a thug too!" the white girl growled when she peeped his swagger. The kids in school may have adopted street nicknames and demeanors but this dude was the real deal.

"Oh lawd!" Marquita laughed when she noticed the white girl staring a dent into her son. "Don't be out here making me no high yella grand babies!"

"I won't mama," he said and cocked a crooked smile at the two girls. Katie may have paid the most attention but Kelondra received most of the reciprocation. She ducked under his gaze until they were gone.

"That must be his girlfriend?" she wondered since mothers didn't look like that in these parts. Marquita could pass for a high schooler on a good day like today.

"I look like his girlfriend!" Katie corrected and licked her lips once more.

The Williams family people watched and window shopped for a few hours before hitting the hardware store. The new house needed lots of new things but window treatments headed the long list. One of the gift certificates left by one of the donors covered the shopping trip. Another paid for lunch and there would be many more to come.

The new school had a championship in view and didn't mind paying for it. The right amount of influence might steer Marquis to the right school for the year required before being drafted. He was already a top ten prospect as a junior. One good year of college could propel him to number one.

But first he had to get through high school. West view high school was a million miles from the hood but that didn't make it necessarily safer.

"Hmp!" Sinclair Rollins huffed as she looked through the blinds. She should have been satisfied that the newspapers had been replaced by proper window treatments. She had intended to tape the rules on the door with the subsection and paragraph highlighted in yellow, but Marquita beat her to it. It didn't but only because nothing could satisfy this fussy woman. Her husband would bend over backwards to please or at least appease, but she would complain he didn't bend over sideways.

"Hmp," her husband agreed with mirth lifting the corner of his mouth. He took it as a victory since he didn't get many.

"Mom, I need two hundred dollars," Carey junior announced since he didn't ask. Not to mention he didn't actually need it since he had thousands of dope dollars in his room. No, he was just spoiled as fuck and expected everything to be handed to him. That's why he directed the demand to his mother, knowing exactly what she would say.

"Dear, give your son two hundred dollars," Mrs said to her Mr. She didn't ask either since it was she who spoiled their child. Now he felt just as entitled as she did.

"The son who just barged into our bedroom, without knocking?" Mr Rollins quipped sarcastically. It was wasted on both peas in the pod who stared back with blank looks on their faces. He had tried to train them to do better but he was the one who was actually trained. As such he knew the sooner he gave in the sooner he could be left alone. "Sure, here..."

"Thanks mom," Carey said as he plucked the bills from his father's hand. Luckily he didn't look in his father's face since the mix of disgust and disappointment could not be missed.

Carey used his phone to start his car as he headed outside. Meanwhile, across the street the William's car wouldn't even start with the key. The two future teammates locked eyes from the distance. Marquis began a nod but Carey had already turned his head, turned his nose up and got into his car.

"Wave him down. We need a jump," Marquita called from the driver's seat. She was no mechanic but by now could pretty well determine which of the raggedy cars many ailments kept it from starting.

"Nah," he said to himself and let him pass. Not that the spoiled brat intended to help anyway.

Carey looked straight ahead until he was far enough to glare through the rearview. Marquis was his competition even if they would be on the same team. He had been the point guard for his whole four years and had no plans on moving over to the two guard spot. Marquis shook his head but he wasn't the only one.

"Where did I go wrong?" Carey senior wondered aloud as he watched his son drive right by people in need. His wife provided an answer by just appearing. "Oh."

"Oh what?" Sinclair asked. She quickly decided she didn't care about whatever the answer was and went on. "I'm going to do a little shopping before the..."

"OK dear," he replied before she finished since he didn't care where she was going or what she was doing. As long as she was away from him it was cool. He finished getting ready for his day and headed out to his car.

"Excuse me!" Marquita nearly demanded as she crossed the street. Five cars passed past and looked but no one stopped to help.

"Yes?" Carey asked and blinked rapidly to filter the glare from all of her pretty. Her clean, natural face was a breath of fresh air from all the beat faces at work and even home. Sinclair wore makeup and designer clothes even around the house.

"We just moved in. My car won't start. He needs to get to school and I..." Marquita fussed until she realized she was fussing. This wasn't his problem or his doing so she softened and continued. "It's our first day. School and job."

"Yes, I know. Marquis Williams, point guard," he smiled and shook Marquis's hand. Being involved in the school had him informed of the big fish they just reeled in.

"Nice to meet you," he replied as practiced. Marquita looked impressed at the new found etiquette. He was always polite but now had the words to match. "This is my mom."

"Mrs Williams," Carey nodded and got down to work. Marquita noticed his strong forearms when he rolled his sleeves up. They went with his chiseled face, plus he smelled great. The car turned over and sputtered to life.

"Yay!" she clapped as he unhooked the jumper cables. Marquis twisted his lips at his mother fawning over the man.

"You have a dead cell. I'll put a new one in when I come home, but you'll need another jump when you shut it off," he explained but she didn't hear a word he said. Too busy looking the sophisticated man up and down and taking him all in. It was more curiosity since she had never been up close and personal with his type. The closest she came was the detective who asked her something about something when Leon got shot.

"OK, thanks," Marquis said on their behalf. He shook his hand again as they went their separate ways.

"WANT me to come inside with you?" Marquita asked and unbuckled her seatbelt so she could.

"You mean like you did on my first day of kindergarten?" he asked with a bright smile. The fond memory put a twinkle in his eye and spread a smile on her face as well.

"Yes!" she sang happily but it was short lived.

"Uh no!" he cracked and cackled as her lips twisted.

"You embarrassed by yo mama? Scared I'm twerk on a table!" she teased back.

"Never that!" he assured her with a straight face. "Now, I am scared this car finna blow up so go on to work. I'll see you at home."

"OK baby," she purred and leaned her cheek in for a kiss. He would never be too old for that and planted a smooch on her jaw.

"Must be his mom!" Kelondra decided since she and Katie were glued on the occupants of the car. The old beater drew their attention since it looked out of place in the lot. That's when they noticed the hunk from the mall and didn't blink.

"Must be because I would have stuck my whole tongue down his throat!" Katie snarled and snapped her teeth like a she wolf.

"And I wonder what would go down your throat?" Kelondra asked and tilted her head as if she didn't know.

"Girl his whole dick!" she howled loud enough to turn heads. She could care less what anyone thought so she added a, "Gawk, gawk" for good measure.

Marquis could feel all eyes on him as he walked into the school. He was on his way to becoming a star so he took it all in stride.

CHAPTER 5

"*C*hile..." Marquita chided herself as she pulled into the parking lot of her new job. She didn't know anything about brokering but one of her son's suitors paved the way.

Technically it was illegal to give high school kids money so they worked around it with favors. Renting the house she could never afford as well as a job she wasn't qualified for was a few of those favors. So were the gift cards in varying amounts to various businesses. She still had a few minutes to spare when she walked briskly into the building.

"Can I help you?" the receptionist asked with her mouth but the look on her face said, 'what are you doing here'. She instantly looked out of place since the women wore tailored pants and skirt suits. Marquita didn't have any so she did her best and she wore her Sunday best instead. That included her bright, blonde church wig. Her good wig.

"Yes, my name is Marquita Williams. I'm 'sposed to start today?" she explained, unsurely. Her mind connected the word brokerage with fixing stuff that was broken but it's a good thing she didn't say that.

"Doing what?" the woman winced. Now she was sure she didn't belong since they didn't wear colorful hair around there.

"Um..." Marquita hummed. Luckily she was saved when one of the managers came through the front door.

"You must be Miss Williams!" she gushed but didn't have to guess since no one had a blonde wig.

"Yes?" she replied, wondering why the woman was so happy to see her.

"I'm Deloris Bankston! My son attends West View high as well. He's on the basketball team!" she cheered as she escorted the woman onto the belly of the brokerage. A few heads lifted curiously at the black woman with blonde hair but most quickly went back to getting their money. Her hair could have been on fire and they would have focused on their money. People who are really about their money don't have time to worry about other people. Gossiping is a broke person's hobby.

"Oh, OK," Marquita replied and looked around. She felt as out of place as she looked with all the suits and pantsuits. The women wore bobs and buns to go with their skirts and heels.

"This is you right here!" Deloris sang when they reached an empty cubicle.

"Oh, OK," she said and took her plush seat. "Um, what I'm 'posed to be doing?"

"Whatever you like! Surf the web, tiktok, whatever!" she sang happily and traipsed off.

"OK then..." Marquita laughed as she hopped online to update her social media accounts. She was getting paid thirty dollars an hour to tiktok, Facebook and YouTube. Life was good.

"Marquis! Over here!" Caleb called and stood. The six foot ten inch teen waved from across the chow hall.

Marquis grabbed his food and headed on over to the table reserved for the basketball team. No one was allowed to sit there even if it was empty. All the teams, groups and cliques had their own space. The world is better when everyone has a place and space.

"Sup," Marquis greeted as almost everyone on the team stood to meet him. Everyone except Carey who side eyed his competition.

"I'm Caleb, but everyone calls me Big Dog!" the center introduced. The rest of the team gave their names and nicknames until all that was left was Carey. "And that's Carey 'C-note' Rollins. All star point guard."

"Sup bro. Looks like me and you in the backcourt huh?" Marquis asked and extended his hand. Carey left him hanging for a second longer than necessary to make his point of being the starting point guard.

"Sup. Look forward to you taking the ball out," he quipped and shook his hand. The rest of the team was excited about the kid who could deliver a state championship but all Carey saw was competition.

"Wherever I'm needed," Marquis said gracefully and shook his hand. He was rated the second best point guard in the whole country so he had no need to compete in the lunchroom.

"Looks like you have a few admirers!" the starting forward laughed and nodded as Katie approached with Kelondra in tow.

"The head, cheerleader!" Big Dog snickered at his own joke. He was one of those people who laughed at everything he said like he was hilarious.

"Is this the new star player?" Katie asked as if she didn't know. His name and picture had been circulating all day. It was only lunch and the junior was better than some of the seniors who had been here four years.

Meanwhile Carey kept a close eye on Kelondra's eyes to make sure they didn't venture over to the new guy. He knew she followed Katie wherever she went. It was Katie who taught her the blow job techniques to keep a boyfriend without fucking.

Kelondra knew she was being watched so she stared straight ahead and didn't look down at Marquis stealing glances at her. Carey missed them since he was locked in on his girlfriend. The rest of the school may have been jocking him, but he wasn't impressed. He was looking forward to after school practice so he could show him up and secure his spot.

"I don't know about star...". Marquis began humbly.

"Thirty points, twelve rebounds and fifteen assists a game!" a nerdy player nicknamed 'Steven A' since he was annoying as fuck just like the real Steven A gushed and fawned.

"Pass him some knee pads already," Carey blurted at his blushing. The team laughed at the gay joke but Marquis tilted his head. He wasn't sure if he should be offended or not since they didn't joke like that in the hood.

"I know someone who doesn't need them..." Big Dog chuckled.

"You should know," Katie smirked and sashayed away. He did know, the whole team knew since they all spent a few minutes in her mouth. The new player just got added to the list whether he knew it or not.

"See you later," Kelondra said and leaned in for a kiss. She took advantage of the moment and stole a glance at Marquis. Only to see him looking back at her. Nothing was said but everything was understood.

"THESE KIDS ARE WEIRD AS FUCK!" was Marquis's initial assessment of his new school and new classmates after his first full day. It was weird as fuck too, watching these rich, suburban kids trying to talk, walk and act like thugs. They were just as obsessed with drugs, music and sex as the inner city school he just came from. The common denominator was the demonic music blasted into their souls day in and day out.

He had exchanged phone numbers with everyone who asked and had a gallery full of various vaginas by the time the final bell had rang. He was definitely looking forward to sampling some or all of them. Especially the pretty pink ones the white girls sent. Even if it was Kelondra who really had his attention.

"Chill bruh!" he laughed to himself at the thought of taking Carey's girl too. It was bad enough he was about to take his point guard position.

Marquis managed to get through his first day of school and headed over to the gym complex. The fact that the school had a whole sports complex was one of the perks that got him here. It and the tacit promises to make his mother's life easier. He would have been recruited from any school on the planet due to his skills. He chose West View to get Marquita out of the hood.

Marquita wanted him out of the hood just as badly. The violence she had become accustomed to had gotten increasingly worse. It was she who shopped her son to the highest bidder to save his life. She would have done it for free but the incentives sure made the difference. She had chosen the school before even bringing him here.

"There he is!" one of the three men cheered when they spotted Marquis approaching. The assistant coach actually had a hard on at the arrival of the kid who could take them to the state championship.

"Hey coach E!" Marquis greeted and shook the head coach's hand before being introduced to the two assistant coaches.

"Good to meet you. This is coach Swartz and coach Calla- han," he said and nodded at the others.

"Oh!" Marquis laughed when he realized one of the men was actually a woman. Coach Callahan had a buzz cut and sports bra to contain her breast but the glance she gave his crotch gave her away. Stud or no stud she was a pretty, yellow woman whether she liked it or not.

"Well, let's get to it," coach E said and led the way inside before he got an erection as well.

"Wow!" Marquis muttered as they stepped inside the multi million dollar sports complex. The last championship banner was from the nineties when Coach E was the point guard.

That wasn't the 'wow' though. The wow was the full cheerleader squad in tiny practice shorts. Ass cleavage jumped and jiggled everywhere as they ran through a routine. They didn't just dance and twerk like the girls from his old school. They did flips and made massive towers like a college team. Most of them would receive scholarships to do just that in colleges around the country. Especially Kelondra who was standing on a girl's hands high above the mat. She did a double flip before being caught by the girls below.

"Damn!" Marquis exclaimed and clapped.

"I know right. That bitch is fine," Coach Callahan snickered and led the way. Now it was her ass that jiggled in her sweatpants that had his attention.

"You fine too," he said under his breath. Not far enough under because she spun and gave him a look. It looked like she was down for whatever hung another championship banner from the wall.

"A'ight guys. Let's get a scrimmage. Rollins runs point for shirts. Williams, skins..." Coach E directed and sat back to take notes.

"Williams on the second team?" assistant coach Swartz asked and got a, 'don't ask me any questions' look for response. "Oh, OK."

All activities came to a screeching halt when Marquis peeled off his practice jersey. Once again Carey shot a glance over to his girlfriend. This Kelondra had joined her cheer team and gawked at the pecs and abs on the new kid. All assumed the bulge in the shorts was all dick. One hoped, another planned to find out as soon as possible.

A nerdy second string guard showed Marquis all of his braces when he inbounded the ball. Marquis didn't know any of the team's plays yet but that was the point. Carey had a point to prove and quickly picked him up as he crossed center court.

Marquis threw a slight juke and Carey bit on it. He was way too determined to show hIm up and overcompensated. Marquis on the other hand had no interest in showing him up. He spared him on the juke move and didn't blow by him. Instead he dished to the forward for a shot jump shot.

"Nice shot! That's you all day!" Marquis cheered and made the kid cheese. The second string was used to getting dragged by the starters and this was the first lead they ever had. Even if it was just 2-0.

"Thanks!" Tank cheesed and high fived him.

"Come on!" Carey barked at the two guard as he took it out. He planned to show off his track and field speed and blow past him. It was the right plan except it would be better if he kept the basketball.

"Woah!" Coach E reeled when Marquis easily picked his pocket and went in for a reverse dunk. The second string went wild since it was now 4-0.

"Calm down! This isn't the championship!" Coach Callahan laughed.

"May as well be," Swartz mentioned since the two guards put on a show. There was a reason Carey was the starter, other than his daddy's money and his mother's influence. The boy could shoot so he shot. The score was quickly 6-4 after a pair of long three pointers.

"I do that too," Marquis replied to the smug look on Carey's face after draining a third three. Carey made the decision to give him a few feet to compensate for his patented juke moves. That proved to be the wrong decision when

Marquis pulled a long three and walked off while the shot was still in the air.

"Nuh-uh...." Callahan said but it was the only words as the whole gym watched the ball sail through the air. A swish broke the silence and the gym went wild.

A video of that shot was uploaded before Carey took the ball out again. They went back and forth but it was a lopsided battle. Marquis got his teammates involved and got them wide open shots. Now Carey wasn't the only starter fighting for his spot. Carey resulted to hard fouls and cheap shots to keep even. Marquis knew he had to keep his composure and did.

The next time up the court would make the coaches decision even easier. Little did Carey know Marquis had set him up all game by playing right handed when he was a natural lefty. He faked right and crossed him over like Iverson did Jordan that one time. Carey tried to cut back but his ankle twisted under the strain. He went down and Marquis went in for another dunk.

The second string had won their first scrimmage ever and Carey lost his spot to the ankle sprain. Half the team celebrated while the other half checked on Carey as the trainers tended to him. Marquis's old school only had a drunken nurse who smelled like pee, while this school had a whole sports medicine team.

"Come here..." someone said and snatched Marquis away from the celebration. Katie snatched him away so hard he couldn't resist if he wanted to.

"Where are we going?" Marquis laughed as she drug him away.

"In here!" she said and she shoved him into the aqua center. The pro hoe knew all the spots to duck off and fuck or suck because she was a hoe. And hoes gonna be alright.

"I ain't even take a shower!" Marquis protested as she

descended in front of him. He was so nervous he wanted to resist.

"That's OK. I prefer a little salt on my meat," she assured and took the sweaty dick into her mouth. There were no further complaints when he touched her tonsils. He leaned back and enjoyed his first taste of white girl head.

CHAPTER 6

"*H*ow was your first day?" Marquita asked when Marquis arrived home. The smirk on his face answered before he did. "Good I see!"

"Great!" he corrected since the white girl head still had him tingly inside. He certainly wouldn't tell her about that so he asked a question of his own. "Where's the car?"

"Chile that thang died at work!" she recalled, shaking her head. She was so embarrassed when the old car sputtered and sparked as once she finally got it started. Luckily she was able to drive it away from the other cars before it caught fire and burned to the ground.

"Wow!" Marquis reeled when she recounted the story.

"Yeah, Mrs Bankston drove me home. Her son plays on your team. Tank?" she recalled. The woman talked her to death over her only child. Tank may have been on the basketball team but that's where his hoop dreams ended. It was just an extracurricular activity to help on his way to medical school.

"Tank is the man!" Marquis nodded. He may be playing on the first string but the second string was his squad. "Coach drove me home."

"Good. He's a nice man," she nodded. "Deloris said one of the boosters was going to let us use a car."

"Booster?" he wondered since the only boosters he knew of stole clothes from the mall.

"See, don't be ghetto!" Marquita chided, even though she had just found out what alumni boosters were herself. The wealthy donors who made sure the school had everything they needed including sports complexes and star athletes like Marquis.

"Oh, OK," he agreed when she explained what was explained to her. Which in turn explained why a car pulled up into the driveway. Another car pulled to a stop on the street but the driver didn't get out.

"That must be who Deloris said was coming over?" Marquita suggested since no one she knew now knew where she lived. Her son was on her heels as she came out to investigate.

"Miss Williams?" the man asked but it really wasn't a question since he didn't wait for an answer. "I work for McNaughton Chevrolet/Volkswagen. I was told to deliver this?"

"I ain't gotta pay nothing do I?" she asked before moving for the shiny key fob he was holding out. "Cuz I just started my job and I ain't got paid yet!"

"No ma'am. No money. Nothing to sign," he assured and extended the keys a little more. The mother looked to her son for confirmation. It came in the form of a nod and she took the key fob.

"Tell Miss Deloris and Mr McNaughton we said thank ya, hear," she said and rushed behind the wheel. Marquis watched the driver hop into the passenger seat of the second car before joining his mother.

"Where we going?" he asked and buckled up.

"Back to the mall. I need some new clothes for work," she decided. Marquita wasn't the sharpest tool in the shed but she didn't need to be to understand the stares she got at work. She didn't dress like the other women did but she had plenty of gift certificates to change that.

"DON'T BE BRANGING HOME a whole bunch of yellow babies now!" Marquita fussed playfully as they pulled back onto their block. She laughed but the fact that she kept reiterating it meant she was serious.

"Ion know what you talmbout mama!" he laughed and played dumb.

"Them dang white gals were all over your ass!" she recalled. Quite a few thought she was his girlfriend but flirted anyway.

"Cuz I'm finna be a star," he sighed and shook his head. He only picked up a basketball after the old timers told him how much he looked like his dad and how good he once was. He was still pretty good on the prison yard but Marquis was destined for greatness.

"Mmhm. I done heard about that white girl head! They say..." she was saying until she saw they had company waiting at the house.

"Uh-oh," Marquis said when he saw the look on Mrs Rollins' face. The whole family had come over to knock on the door but it was clear the Mrs led this mission. Carey junior wore an orthopedic boot on his foot and leaned on his new crutches.

"Something happened in school?" she asked even though there wasn't enough time to hear the story since she was pulling in. They had been down this road before when Marquis beat up a classmate or two.

"Well..." he replied and looked at the Rollins family. The father and son's head's were both lowered in both submission of her, plus the fact they didn't want to be here.

"Hey, can I help you?" Marquita asked as calmly as she could.

She even willed her neck to stay still but a little sass still seeped out.

"Your son shoved my son and made him twist his ankle!" Sinclair insisted to both Carey's surprise. They looked at each other but didn't dare speak up. One was a puppet and the other was whipped by the pussy he rarely got to visit. She pointed her finger inches from Marquis's face so he looked to his mother.

"OK first, the finger? Un-uh," she said and politely moved it from her son's face. Then turned to him for his side of the story. "Well?"

"I ain't push him mama! I hit him with the juke and he twisted his ankle," he explained. The Rollins men looked even more embarrassed at the explanation. Marquita stifled a smirk since she had seen that juke move drop a hundred opponents over the years. They were lucky her son didn't break Carey's ankle like a few of Marquis's other victims. Poor Sinclair was the only one who didn't know what was going on.

"Hit him with a, juke?" she wondered. No one wanted to explain so she took flight without an explanation. "Why did he bring a juke to school? This isn't the hood! I should call the police..."

"Come on Sinclair..." Mr Rollins finally spoke up and he steered his wife back across the street. Carey junior refused to look up or offer the apology he owed. He just used his new crutches and hopped along behind his parents. The Williams family watched them cross the street before looking at each other. Then cracked up.

"Don't brang that juke to school no mo! She gonna call the cops!" Marquita cackled as they retreated back into the house.

"THAT SUCKS!" Kenneth moaned when Carey hopped in the den on his crutches.

"Tell me about it," he sighed. They both had to be themselves since Kenneth and Kelondra's mother was present.

"I'll let you guys talk..." Mrs Cheshire said and stood. Carey pressed his lips together to form a sort of smile, then locked in on her ass as she walked out. It was clear where Kelondra got all that ass from, even if she had a long way to go to catch up with her mother.

"Bruh..." Kenneth complained since no man wants to see anyone gawking at his mom's ass.

"I'm saying tho..." Carey finally laughed. It was the first laugh of the week after getting embarrassed at practice and put on crutches.

"Saying what?" Kelondra asked as she made her appearance. She changed into a pair of tiny shorts when she saw Carey's car pull into the driveway. She really could be sued for false advertising since all that ass she was slinging was still untouched.

"Private shit!" he snapped back hard enough for Kenneth to frown. First his mother's ass, now acting an ass with his sister.

"Let's bounce," he said and stood. That was the extent he would stand up to his domineering friend though. His sister twisted her lips and wondered if he shouldn't be wearing the shorts. Since he was a bitch and all.

"Yeah," Carey agreed and pulled himself up on his crutches. He was still in a salty mood so he cheated himself out of watching Kelondra's ass as she stomped off. Kenneth mentally popped his collar and took credit for the slight check about looking at his mother. Both suburban kids had transformed into their alter egos by the time they reached the car.

"Check this one..." Keto cheered and produced a different gun.

"Sweet! Mama got some new heat!" C-note noted since they usually toted Mrs Cheshire's guns when they went down into the city to re-up.

"Hell naw, this is me!" he declared triumphantly. All the

rappers they looked up to had guns of their own but he had been sneaking his mom's.

"Where the hell did you get a gun from?" C-note dared and cocked his head dubiously. That was the condescending attitude that made Keto keep it to himself until he pulled it off.

"It's a ghost gun! I ordered the parts and had it assembled!" he explained. He saw the glimmer of jealousy in his friend's eye and smiled.

"Well, order another. This one is mine," he declared and took the gun away. Keto pouted the rest of the way to the hood. His sister was right about the shorts. C-note tucked the pistol into his pants and got out. He had a whole new swag that had nothing to do with the crutches. The heavy gun in his waist was like a set of iron balls.

"Come on!" Man-man called from his usual spot on the sofa. The old sofa now had a deep groove that fit his ass to a tee.

"Sup shawty!" Keto cheered as he led the way into the apartment. Scooter just burst out laughing while C-note shook his head.

"Y'all niggas some dope boys for real!" Man-man exclaimed happily, then stifled a laugh at the looks on their faces. These dudes were some pretenders but they spent good money with him.

"Y'all need to get some dih right chere..." Scooter said from the dinette table. C-note shook his head but curiosity pulled Keto over like a magnet does metal.

"Crack!" he cheered like it was the answer to a trivia question.

"Hell yeah. I'll let y'all get it for, two bands an ounce," Scooter nodded at the outrageous markup he made up. Man-man couldn't not laugh this time. Ounces sold for five hundred dollars all day long in the hood.

"That's you right there..." Man-man said and nodded at the

bag containing their re-up. He laughed again when C-note limped over to retrieve it.

"What?" C-note barked when he saw him looking at the boot on his foot. No one from anywhere likes being laughed at. His tone put Scooter on alert since it was the type of tone that keeps funeral homes in business.

"Naw, nothing. Just saw that video of my boy Marquis put that juke on you!" he said and laughed some more. Keto twisted his mouth and tried not to laugh. He had seen the video himself but didn't dare bring it up. Not to mention Kelondra had to witness it and had received the cold shoulder ever since.

"You got that," he nodded and smiled through the malice. They completed the deal and he turned to leave before stopping for one final question. "Say, can you do a hundred pounds?"

"Hell yeah!" Man-man shot back. He was so excited about the huge profit he stood to make that he almost stood up. "When do you want it?"

"I'll let you know..." C-note said and hobbled away.

"Bruh, you really ready to spend that much?" Keto reeled once they were back in the car. Neither seemed to notice the thirsty looks on the young faces looking at them. It was only Man-man's status in the complex that prevented them from being robbed.

"Hell naw," he replied and cocked his head at his own sinister idea. Keto waited but wouldn't get an explanation. His shoulders shrugged since he had a few ideas of his own. First was ordering a new ghost gun.

CHAPTER 7

"Take this over to them folks house," Marquita said and held out a plate of hot BBQ, fresh off the grill. She resisted all temptation and didn't invite anyone from the old hood to her cookout.

Her cookouts used to attract quite the crowd in her apartments. There would be music, Spades, dominoes and dancing. Couples might couple up and sneak off to fuck. The weed and alcohol would flow freely until someone got into an argument with someone else. Then a fight, then the gun shots would run everyone inside like a flash rain shower. Her head nodded in agreement with the decision to keep it just between her and her son. Their new life was no place for their old friends.

"What folk?" Marquis asked indignantly and didn't move for the heavy plate she held out. It was piled high with ribs, chicken and the cheap cuts of steak she could get with her stamps. She would cook them low and slow until they were nice and tender. That's why she bought the same cuts now even when he had gift certificates for the supermarket as well.

"Yo teammate and his daddy," she snickered. Mr Rollins was

a handsome man but he was married. This was a peace offering so they could live in peace. "I guess his mama can eat too."

"But still..." he said and moved his hands behind his back to indicate he had no intentions on taking the plate over to the Rollin's home.

"Boy!" she fussed and shook her head. Peace requires sacrifices so she removed her apron to make one. "I'll take it over there my dang self!"

Removing the apron probably wasn't the best idea for burying the hatchet since her little shorts hugged her fine frame tighter than a scared child hugs its mother. They just barely managed to hold all that ass inside but nestled up in her crotch and showed that fat rabbit beneath. It was clearly rabbit season, have those shorts tell it.

"Good," Marquis laughed and dug in. He grabbed one of the steaks and pulled it apart with his fingers. He did keep an eye on his mama as she went over just in case. That Carey kid was weird as far as he was concerned. They saw each other in school in the days since the incident at practice but he still hadn't spoken. Even at the same lunch table with the whole team.

"Be nice!" Marquita told herself as she approached the Rollins home. She had to reaffirm herself when the door opened and Sinclair Rollins stepped out. She stopped in her tracks and lifted her designer shades to make sure she saw what she was seeing. "Hey there Mi Rollins, I..."

"Tuh!" Sinclair huffed before the woman could finish saying whatever she was saying. Instead she hopped in her vehicle and hit the locks like white folks do black folks when they see them coming. Marquita almost thought it was a joke until she almost got hit by the car as she sped from the driveway.

"Are you OK!" Mr Rollins pleaded as he rushed outside. He had been watching from the window so he could pull up his favorite porn once his wife was gone.

"Ion know what her problem is!" Marquita snarled as he

looked her over to make sure she was ok. His eyes got pulled between her legs just like the itty bitty shorts were.

"I um?" he asked when he pried his eyes from her vagina print. "Um?"

"I'm fine. She missed me," she cooed, flattered from the way he looked at her. Leon could sometimes look at her like a piece of meat since she was just a piece of ass to him. This man looked at her like a piece of art and she liked it.

"Thank you. I mean, thank goodness. God, thank God," he stammered and flattered her some more. In the hood dudes just grimaced and said, 'damn', 'shit', and 'fuck'.

"Well, we cooked out so I wanted to offer you guys a plate?" Marquita offered and extended the plate.

"Wow, thanks!" Mr Rollins cheered genuinely. He could see spare ribs poking through the aluminum foil and didn't bother to inform her that the Rollins family didn't eat pork. Mainly because Mrs Rollins didn't and didn't allow it. Both Carey's would when they could get away with it.

"You're so welcome. And, thanks for helping with the car the other day," she smiled.

"My pleasure," he said as his eyes dropped to her chest and back up. He had hoped she didn't but the sly smirk suggested she did.

"OK then.." Marquita gave a nod and turned to walk away. Married or not, she knew he was glued on her ass so she gave him something to look at. Revenge for his Mrs who nearly ran her over. He felt himself stiffening in his boxer briefs.

"Sinclair would lose her mind if she saw these ribs..." he offered as an excuse. This meant devouring them the way he did was a favor to his wife. His uppity wife would never allow him to cook out like this since she declared this kind of food beneath them.

"Negro food!" he laughed and chomped into the tender ribs. The sweet sauce covered his face and made him even happier.

He knocked off the pork and put the bones in a bag to dispose of. His son was just as uppity as his mother so he ate the chicken too. Then the steak, until the plate was clean. He folded the plate under the foil and into the bag. "Nigga need a nap now!"

Carey senior intended to take a good nap while his nagging wife and whiney son were out of the house. The porn would have to wait for another time. He washed the BBQ sauce from his mouth and face before hitting the bed. The sound of water and laughter wafted above before he could drift away. He already knew the voice before he got back up to investigate.

"Take that!" Marquita squealed as she sprayed her son with the water hose. Their playful antics while washing the family car was unusual in the stuffy neighborhood.

"Keep that same energy mama!" he laughed back and tossed the bucket of sudsy water on her.

"You got that!" she conceded. They got back to the business of actually washing the car. Meanwhile Carey Rollins was stuck like Chuck with a buck in a truck with bad luck.

The water had virtually dissolved her tank top and put her heavy breast on full display. A display that was just as good when she turned since her ass cheeks hung from the bottom of the shorts. Carey senior was so hard he got a little light headed. He wasn't even aware of how his erection found its way into his hand.

"This isn't right," he muttered when he caught himself stroking himself. He wasn't talking about the part of jacking off while peering from a window at the neighbor. No, he meant not having his trusty lube in his palm as he did it.

Carey rushed to his office and squeezed some into his hand. He arrived back at the window just as she bent over to wash the rims. The plump mound of pussy between her legs could be seen from the back. That was enough to send the electric currents shooting throughout his body. Marquita happened to turn and look in that direction. She couldn't see him but it was enough to kick him over the edge.

"Ugh! Fuck!" he grunted and groaned as she skeeted on the new drapes. In a further act of defiance he cleaned his dick with them and laid down. This was the best nut and nap he had in a long time.

"GAME TIME!" Coach Callahan cheered as the players entered the gymnasium. She was so excited she acted more like a cheer-leader than a coach. Her barely used box moistened a bit at the prospect of a state championship.

"Sup coach!" Marquis greeted and raised his hand for a high five.

"Un-uh, bring it in!" she insisted and stole a hug.

"Um, OK," he laughed. It was slightly awkward until he noticed this manly chick was all chick. She smelled like a woman and felt so soft he started to get hard.

"Oh!" the coach reeled when she felt the lump form against her. She reeled but didn't budge.

"Uh, I gotta go stretch and get ready, for the um, game," Marquis said as he wiggled out of her clutches.

"Oh, yeah! Yeah. Stretch, warm up!" she insisted like it was her idea.

"Shiiiiit, I'd hit that," he mumbled as he rushed into the building. He did need to stretch and warm up but first things first.

"In here!" Katie said and snatched him into an empty room. She promised him another blow job but had a change of plans.

"Damn, white girl!" Marquis exclaimed with a grimace when he saw she was completely naked. He had never seen a naked white girl before and she didn't disappoint.

"Figured we could do something different?" she suggested

suggestively. They had met up all week for blow jobs but tonight was game night. What better way to get loose than getting some pussy.

He whipped out a rock hard dick for a reply and searched his wallet for a condom. Katie dipped low and gave him an appetizer as he bit the package open. She laid back while he rolled the rubber on the wood and took position between her thighs.

Katie let out a hiss and scrunched her face as he eased inside. She was still young enough to be good and tight but all this fucking was going to catch up with her one day. Not this day though and her young box gripped that dick like a python grips its dinner.

He obviously forgot about all that dick she sucked because when she leaned up for a kiss he met her halfway. He twirled his tongue in her mouth and gripped her alabaster ass cheeks. The sounds of squishy sex reverberated around the room but it wouldn't for long.

"Damn, white girl!" Marquis moaned as his stroke grew choppy.

"Mmhm," she hummed and squeezed. That did the trick causing him to seize and fill the condom up.

"Fuck!" he declared and reluctantly pulled out. He didn't even remove the rubber before pulling his pants back up.

"Now go drop sixty on them!" the cheerleader cheered as he rushed from the room. Katie cleaned herself up and put her cheerleader uniform back on. They wouldn't see each other again until game time.

"YOU DON'T HAVE to come if you're not ready!" Sinclair Rollins declared to her pouty son in the back seat.

'That's why he's a little bitch now!' Mr Rollins screamed, but only in his mind. He was a spoiled brat and she was the one who spoiled her.

"Gotta support my team," Carey replied. At least the boot on his feet and crutches gave him an excuse for losing his starting spot.

"Good choice son," Carey senior spoke up. His eyes scanned the parking lot for a spot and missed his wife and son rolling their eyes. He did see Marquita pulling into a parking spot in front of them. That's why he attempted to turn the other direction.

"Where are you goings stupid!" Sinclair snapped. She had gotten so used to disrespecting him it came naturally. "There's empty spots right there! And your son is on crutches..."

"Yes dear," he said even though she wasn't finished fussing. She fussed at him until she saw something else to fuss about.

"There's that, woman!" Sinclair spat and literally spat on the ground. The entire Rollins clan watched Marquita's round ass shift in a pair of skin tight jeans. "She had the audacity to attempt to bring us a plate of her ghetto food!"

"The nerve!" Mr Rollins reeled while thinking, 'them shits were delicious'. He had to avert his eyes from the ass when he felt his dick begin to stiffen.

"I'm going to sit with the team," Carey moped and hobbled over to the bench. His mother pouted as his dilemma while his father twisted his lips. He had sprained his ankle plenty times growing up and never had a boot or crutches.

"C-note!" Big Dog cheered as his teammate hobbled over. Everyone stood and exchanged dap including Marquis but he got ignored.

"Sit with me," Callahan offered and patted the empty seat next to her. It would be the only seat with an actual ass in it once the game began. Because the new recruit showed his ass and did drop sixty points on their opponents. Marquis added twelve rebounds, four steals and fourteen assists in a well-rounded game. Carey junior was the only face in the place not cheering. Instead he jeered as the crowd and cheerleaders mobbed the star player.

"Nice game!" Kelondra gushed and batted her eyes when they caught his.

"Thanks..." he said and settled for that, for now. There was so much more he wanted to say but it would have to wait.

"Hey baby!" Carey announced and gripped Kelondra's ass for show. He snatched her up and forced a kiss on her.

"Um hey," she said uncomfortably and looked around to make sure her mom wasn't watching. She wasn't, since her dad showed up with his new girlfriend. Her mother was too busy watching them. "Are you OK?"

"I will be..." he said as he watched Marquis head into the locker room. He waved to her brother and left her standing alone.

CHAPTER 8

"*J*on know 'bout 'di!" Marquita moaned when her son emerged from his room.

"It's just a party mama!" Marquis chuckled.

"Yeah, but these white folks. They party, party!" she complained. Parties in the hood usually ended in someone getting their ass whooped or killed. White parties ended up in overdoses and pregnancies.

"It's cool mama. I'm still the same me," he assured. It was comforting since she knew she raised him right. She quit drinking and smoking weed when she missed that first period after conceiving him. It's a whole lot easier to keep a kid from behavior they see their parents doing.

The whole, 'do as I say, not as I do' is a hot pile of steamy, hypocritical horse shit. Kids are going to be what they see. Mainly from the ones they are supposed to follow the most. Which is why these rich black and white kids drank, smoked and popped all kinds of pills. Why wouldn't they when they see it every day?

"Mmhm. Don't make no babies tonight!" she fussed. If

anyone knew that chicks trap dudes with babies it would be her. She tried to trap his trap star daddy by getting pregnant on him. It worked but the police trapped him too and sent him away for a couple decades.

"I'm pretty sure I won't mom!" he assured her confidently. These rich suburban girls swallowed and you can't make a baby like that.

"Well, you bet not wreck my shit either!" she fussed and dangled the key fob on her big ass key chain.

"Mama..." he dared and cocked his head. He had been doing most of the driving since he got his permit. He kissed her cheek and headed out the door. Marquis and Carey both came out at the same time. He tried to nod a 'what's up' but Carey turned his head before he could. He shrugged and got into his mother's car. He pulled out behind him and followed him to the party.

"Damn!" Marquis exclaimed when they reached the cul de sac that held the party house. Cars lined the block from both corners. The party had spilled out into the front yard. Carey pulled his Audi onto the front lawn and went inside.

Marquis parked near the corner and began to walk over to the party house. He saw the party had spilled into several parked cars that doubled as motels. At least three were bouncing up and down while thirst quenching blow jobs occupied a few more.

"These white kids shole know how to party!" he laughed and made his way inside.

"Grand Marquis!" Big Dog shouted when Marquis entered the house.

"Sho nuff," he laughed at his new nickname. It sure beat the 'booga' his granny used to call him.

"Over here!" he waved him over to where the team was posted up. All except C-note who was making his rounds, selling his weed.

"Good game!" was echoed all around the circle. They had

been destroyed by that same team last year but now they won by nearly thirty points.

"Thanks. No thanks," he said, accepting the praise while declining the drugs and alcohol they passed around. He kept an eye on the pool filled with bikinis. Booties and boobies bounced along with the music banging from the system. Topless teens had him mesmerized.

"Whew!" the teams forward proclaimed as he burst from the pool house. Katie came out behind him, wiping her mouth. Marquis had been looking forward to seeing her but now acted like he didn't see her. He turned his head to see Kelondra staring back. They shared a quick smile before Carey came up behind her.

"Mmhm!" he laughed and spun her around to face him.

"Hey there!" Kelondra cheesed. Carey had been distant and cold lately so she was happy to see him happy.

"See you dick riding again!" he said through the same smile.

"Huh? Who? I ..." she reeled but he walked away. She tilted her head as Carey pushed up on a white girl named Roslyn. When she looked away there was Marquis looking back. Nothing was said but everything was understood.

"I can't believe you don't wanna get this money!" Keto complained once again.

"Believe it! We don't need to sell crack!" C-note shot back. "Who we gonna sell it to anyway? Ain't no crack heads at West View."

"Not yet! I saw a movie where they gave out testers. Free testers to let 'em get a taste, then they hooked!" he declared cheerfully as if hooking their classmates on crack was something to cheer about.

"I saw that movie too! I loved when they got into that

shootout..." C-note fondly recalled. Most of their new personas came from movies and music.

"So, you wanna do it?" Keto pleaded.

"Nah, we good on the weed." C-note decided firmly. His partner just nodded his head but not in agreement. "Anyway, look what Roslyn sent me..."

"Nice!" he said of the pretty vagina on the screen. He turned the phone sideways because vaginas look good from the side too. Then enlarged it because vaginas look even better close up. "Wait, why is she sending this to you? Everyone knows you and Kelondra are dating!"

"Cuz, I'm a playa, playa!" he laughed. Keto didn't laugh along with him since he didn't like it. "Chill bruh. I'm not leaving my girl but you know she won't put out."

"Bruh, that's my sister!" he grimaced since he didn't want to think about anyone doing to his sister what he does to other people's sisters.

"And she don't put out! Shit, you should want me fucking Roslyn and everyone else who isn't Kelondra!" he reasoned. The pause indicated that Keto was going for it so he brought it home. "Or you just want all the white girls for yourself? You like Tiger Woods our thi bih!"

"Since you put it that way..." Keto agreed since he didn't want his friend or anyone fucking his sister. Good thing he didn't know Kelondra gave some mean head. That was the reason for the smirk on his friend's face.

"Good, so keep it to yourself," C-note said and produced a thick joint. They blazed it and got blazed before their next stop.

The couple of wannabe thugs collected their money and divided the proceeds. Minus what would be spent on re-up they each had plenty of money to floss and toss like the ballers did in the videos.

"You're not coming in?" Keto asked on behalf of his sister. She had been moping around for a few days after the party.

Kelondra kept asking about him so he knew his friend was the cause of her melancholy.

"Nah..." he said with a smirk since Kelondra had appeared at the front door.

"Really?" Kelondra fussed as he backed out of the driveway while locking eyes. Carey was back to playing basketball but their relationship was just as strained. He still resented Marquis even though his numbers had improved playing the two guard. Carey benefitted from the assist and double team plays opponents employed, but a hater is gonna hate. It's just what they do. "Two can play that game..."

"Hello?" Marquis asked curiously when he took a call from the unknown number. Most of the numbers in his phone had either a face, name or vagina attached to it.

"Oh, now you don't know me?" Kelondra fussed.

"Kelondra?" he asked, catching the voice. They hadn't exchanged numbers but she made it her business to get it. Then made it her business to get to know him.

"OK THEN!" Marquita laughed triumphantly when she checked her accounts at work. Deloris may have been content with her posting content to her social media accounts while on the clock but she was determined to learn the business.

Marquita looked over shoulders , asked questions and learned the business on her own time. An older white man took her under his wing and taught her all about the business of making money from other people's money.

She didn't stop there and learned to talk like they talked and walk like they walked. In a few months she didn't 'taw 'li 'thi, anymore. Plus she dressed like they dressed and stopped changing hair color every other day.

Marquita did still wear her booty shorts while washing the

car. And Mr Rollins still posted up where she couldn't see him and pulled on his penis. She also made sure to bring him a plate whenever his wife and son's car's weren't in the driveway. Which was quite often which gave them time to get to know each other better.

Both stayed cognizant of the line between them and didn't cross. Both were starved for attention and fed off of each other. Ironically neither understood most of what the other was saying at first. Soon he knew who each of these rappers and entertainers were and she knew a little about the politics and world events he often spoke of.

"I'm finna take Carey a plate..." Marquita announced as she watched Carey junior drive away. Sinclair had left an hour ago for her bridge game which gave them a few hours to talk.

"OK," Marquis grunted to whatever she just said since he was more interested in what Kelondra was saying. They spoke daily and deep into the night but never tried to meet up. Sometimes it's good to have friends who don't want anything from you. Even when you would take and give everything if the chance arose.

"Well, hey there Miss Williams," Carey senior greeted casually. So casually it gave no hint of the good nut he bust while she washed the windows.

"Mr Rollins," she replied with a nod and smile. The formalities made them both think their purely platonic relationship was OK. It really wasn't since it was really still a relationship. He accepted the plate and dug in. Marquita fondly watched the man enjoy her food until the plate was cleared. They spent the next hour going back and forth between TMZ and CNN.

"Shit, I'm about to get this bread!" Kenneth decided and stood. It was him who dipped into the closet but he emerged as Keto since his ghost gun was on his hip. He counted out twenty grand to spend and made a call to the hood.

"Yeah!" Scooter barked since he was busy. Busy or not he answered his business phone when it rang. Even while giving some young hood rat the business.

"Uh, hello?" Keto asked unsurely, since it sounded like he reached a porn set.

"Nigga, you just, called, me!" the thug demanded with each thrust. The young girl moaned with each one so Keto had to speak over her.

"Di uh, Keto, 'ndem. I uh, wanna get some rock. Crack rock?" he asked.

"You, gone have to hit, me, back!" he said with the back shots echoing in the background. The teen girl had just recently jumped off the porch so he had to have his way with before the streets and strip clubs got hold to her. This tight little box would never be like this again after that. Still, he needed to know, "How much you tryna spend?"

"I got a dove. Dub, I mean dub. Yeah, twenty brands," he struggled. His slang was like foreigner's English. Right words, wrong context.

"Hey!" the girl shrieked when he abruptly snatched the dick from her insides. He had one foot in his pants already.

"Come on!" he shouted at the easy lick. Twenty thousand could get a whole kilo but he only had a few ounces.

"I'm gonna be like forty minutes," Keto said since he was just leaving the house.

"Oh, OK," Scooter said and pulled his leg from his pants. Forty minutes gave him enough time to finish knocking her off and rounding up enough work to sell him. All it would take was a few more ounces since he wouldn't know any better. A better, more sinister idea came to mind just before he hung up. "Don't go to Man-man house. Just hit back when you get close."

"Oh, OK," Keto agreed since he didn't know any better. He hung up and turned the music up for the ride downtown.

CHAPTER 9

"So, what's your girl gonna say about you stopping by?" Roslyn teased as she let C-note into her home. They had flirted for weeks and finally got a chance to hook up.

"Don't know," he answered honestly since he was still giving Kelondra the cold shoulder since Marquis twisted his ankle and took his spot. The snub put the spoiled teen in a dark place but she got the worst of it.

"Don't care," she snickered and led him up the stairs to her room. Roslyn, like most girls, was jealous of Kelondra. Not only did she come from a wealthier family but she was smart, pretty and still had an intact hymen. They couldn't compete with her academically so they fucked her boyfriend every chance they got. A task made easier by her virginity and his privileged attitude. He was once the prize since he was the star of the basketball team. Not so much lately since Marquis came along.

Kelondra heard the rumors but still one upped the competition since she was the only one he claimed publicly. She got dinners, movies and proms. All they got was the dick. The same dick she stopped sucking when she heard how he was sharing it like a meme. High school was almost over and they would go their separate ways, to different colleges. Once upon a time Kelondra knew she and Carey would marry, have lots of babies and live happily ever after. Now she was certain she wouldn't. In fact, she didn't even like him anymore.

"Do you have any coke?" Roslyn whispered even though the house was empty. Even she knew cocaine was a big step in the wrong direction, she wanted to keep it a secret from herself. And would become a full fledged junkie before she got the news.

"Naw," he snarled since it was bad news. More and more kids had been asking which made it a good business move. He let out a sigh and acquiesced that his friend was right. He would call Keto after he finished here and set up a buy. Not knowing the kid was cruising downtown at that very moment to cop some coke on his own.

"Awe, I would have sucked your dick so good!" she pouted and poked out her lip.

"That's OK. You still can," he comforted and produced the dick. He was right and she did. Sucked it so good he had to beg her to stop. Most of his classmates gave head, including Kelondra. Now they were fucking except for Kelondra. He pried the dick away and laid her back on her princess bed. Then fucked her like a slave.

It was beyond pleasure when he relished in her pain. Most of these teens just started fucking and had brand new vaginas. It gave him great pleasure to inflict pain on them. Carey fucked her as hard and fast as he possibly could. All she could do was grimace, grip the sheets and hope he climaxed quickly. She was still too new and too tight to squeeze the pussy and help him along. So she just had to take it.

"Take that! Take it!" he shouted and picked up the pace. Her box would be swollen and out of commission by the time he finished. His stroke grew choppy which meant the end was near.

"Give it to me!" she shouted, but only because she knew it was almost over. He tipped onto his tippy toes and pushed down to the bottom of her box and let go.

"Argh! Fuck! Shit! Whew!" he groaned, growled and grinded as he filled up the latex. His plan was to bust a nut and bounce so he could catch up with Keto. Enough kids asked for coke to change his mind.

"Oh no you don't!" Roslyn protested when he tried to pull out. "Where do you think you're going? My parents are gone all night. That means I have you, all night."

"Sounds like a plan," he agreed since no guy is going to argue about leaving some pussy to hang out with another guy. Unless, both those guys are gay. Neither was so he would stay put. "Let me hit Keto and let him know I'll see him tomorrow."

"Mmhm," she purred and pulled out her own phone while he worked his. He was able to snap off a few photos of her naked to attach to the text.

'She has some good-good, wet-wet, so I'll see you tomorrow' he sent along with the pictures of her tits and ass.

'Just smashed C-note Rollins. #gooddick' she texted a friend along with his pic and dick.

❦

"NICE!" Keto said when he looked at the pictures and text message. He knew his friend would be tied up for the rest of the night so he didn't bother replying. Instead he called Scooter to let him know he made it downtown.

"Sup shawty!" Scooter blurted on the first ring. He was so excited about the easy lick he bounced in his seat. He had spent this twenty grand in his mind seven times since he finished smashing the young girl. None of it was going to her or his mama or either of his baby mamas.

"I'm um, on Peachtree," he said like that said something. There are five hundred Peachtree something streets in the city of Atlanta.

"Meet me at the gas station across from the S&S on Ashby!" he said since there's only one Ashby street.

"On the way," Keto said and entered it into his GPS. The new Benze was barely noticed on Peachtree but turned every head in the hood.

It was a good thing Scooter was already waiting for him because someone would definitely carjack him if he had to wait. Probably not necessarily a bad thing either since Scooter was on some fuck shit himself too. He startled Keto when he popped out of nowhere and knocked on the window.

"Ugh!" Keto reeled from the start. He relaxed when he saw the familiar face and hit the lock.

"Where the money shawty?" Scooter asked greedily and looked around. Any hood nigga would have known something was wrong but Keto, Kenneth Worthington was no hood nigga.

"Right here, I..." he was saying until a brilliant flash of light lit up the interior of the car. The gunshot that accompanied the light didn't even register through the pain. The bullet had torn through Keto's face and nearly tore his bottom jaw off when it came out the other side.

Scooter grabbed the bag of cash and made the dash. He wisely parked a few blocks away since the station had cameras everywhere. The hoodie and shades made sure all they got was a black male in a hoodie and shades. Keto managed to open the car door and stumbled out onto the asphalt. Two men approached quickly when he laid out and looked up.

He tried to speak but his jaw was barely hanging on. It just dangled dangerously as the men stepped over him to get into the car. Keto heard his tires chirp as he got robbed a second time in one night. The next set of footsteps approaching sounded promising to the wounded man.

"Urghmph," he pleaded to the two teens about his age.

"What's wrong shawty..." one asked but it wasn't really a question since he didn't care. He wouldn't have dug into his pockets looking for loot had he genuinely cared about his well being.

"Shawty got them Js!" the other proclaimed as he peeled the expensive sneakers from his feet.

"Dis nigga scrapped!" the first one declared when his rummaging came across the pistol. He actually meant to say 'strapped' but missed quite a bit of school. Now for the rest of his life he would roam screets, eat scrawberries and scrimp.

"Urghmph" Keto repeated in protest as the kid tried to take the gun. There was a struggle over the ghost gun until it discharged and turned Keto into a ghost. He had been robbed for a third time in one night. This last one took his life along with his property. Luckily the robbers left his phone since they knew too many niggas in the chain gang for stealing a phone that led the police right to them.

"WELL, he's not from around here..." detective Adams surmised at first glance of the newly deceased. Latisha Adams was the newest addition to Atlanta's busy homicide division. Her partner stood back to let her take lead, but also trace the panty lines through her slacks.

"How can you tell?" Jacoby Johnson inquired. He would have come to the same conclusion but it would take more than a glance.

"Socks," she replied. She had a teenaged son at home herself and recognized the expensive socks on the victim's feet. Even his clothes weren't the typical quality most of their victims wore around here.

"Wallet..." the medical examiner announced and retrieved it from his pocket.

"I was thinking robbery?" Latisha asked since she wasn't so sure anymore.

"Still is. They wanted something else from..." Johnson said and paused to read the name from the license. "Kenneth Worthington."

"Definitely not from around here. We Jacksons, Johnsons and Smiths around here," Latisha offered lightheartedly.

"No phone?" Johnson asked hopefully since the world's dumbest criminals like to incriminate themselves on stolen phones.

"Phone," the medical examiner said and handed it over. It was locked but would easily be unlocked back at the precinct.

"Let's go watch the movie." Latisha suggested.

"Let's," Johnson agreed and let her lead the way into the store so he could watch her ass do its little dance in her pants. The woman knew it too and tried to stiffen her walk but a booty does as a booty does. And an ass that fat couldn't be contained.

"Welcome back," the Iraqi clerk announced and waved through the upgraded bullet proof glass. The old glass did fine for decades against the 380s and 38s the hood once favored. Now these goons shot ARs, AKs and MPs, so they had to beef up the protection.

"Welcome back is right," she sighed. They had been here twice this week already. Those homicides were already solved due to the high tech security cameras they installed. It was indeed like watching a movie since the quality was so good.

"Let's see what we got Habib," Johnson said as the clerk let them into the booth. That was his nickname for anyone of Arab descent.

"That would be racist if that wasn't really my name," the

72

clerk sighed and logged into the security system. He caught the tail end of the incident so he knew what time to pull up.

"Nice car," Latisha nodded and went back to a robbery. A dude was robbed and killed last week for his twenty year old BMW so the brand new Benz was definitely a target.

"There's our boy..." Johnson said as the hooded figure emerged from the side. They watched as he looked around and knocked on the window. "Hmp?"

"Yeah, he lets him in! He knows him!" Latisha stated like captain obvious.

"Drug deal gone bad?" Habib offered from over their shoulders. They both shot him a STFU glance and he STFU. "Sorry."

"Damn!" Latisha grimaced when a flash painted the driver's window red. They expected to see Kenneth get pushed out of the car onto the spot he was still laying but the shooter hopped out with a bag he didn't have when he hopped in. "Hmp?"

"Robbery," Johnson nodded and kept watching. They watched as their latest victim fell out of the car and pleaded for help.

"That's cold!" the lady cop declared as two men stepped over Kenneth and drove off with the car. "Robbed twice in two minutes..."

"Make that three times," Johnson said since the victim on the camera still had his shoes on. Nor did he have the hole in his chest that put him into the past tense.

"Here comes number three," Habib said as the last teens appeared on the screen. He almost got another stfu until he offered what he had. "Bay-bay and Ray-ray. They're always around, stealing whatever they can get their hands on."

"Looks like they just got their hands on a murder charge," Latisha said as Ray-ray ended up shooting Kenneth on camera. Bay-bay didn't touch the gun but just caught himself a murder charge all the same.

"I'll put an APB on the car," Johnson said and did just that. It would be just a matter of time until the GPS led police right to it.

"That's the easy part," Latisha sighed and removed the CD with the incident. Now came the part she dreaded most about her job. It was time to notify the next of kin about the death of their loved one.

CHAPTER 10

"*L*et me see you?" Marquis asked and smiled.

"You just seen me in school! I look just the same," Kelondra quipped. She was fronting though because she was scrolling through the pictures she just took for him.

"True, I just like looking at you. You think niggas in the Louvre pass by Mona Lisa and don't look, err time?"

"You silly!" she giggled and blushed. Ironically most of the suburban girls loved his hood but she loved how he wasn't hood at the exact same time. Being hood can be a mindset or a location. Being born and raised in the hood was just a coincidence since he was worldly and learned.

"You're beautiful!" he said as the first of a flurry of pictures began to come through. He had a gallery full of vaginas but her smile topped them all. A sultry selfie in a tank top was as much as she revealed.

"Thank you!" she squealed, gushed and blushed. A sigh quickly followed since Carey never told her that anymore. He was once the sweetest guy until C-note came out. Lately he had become a real prick. The only reason she had been on the phone for hours with Marquis was because he didn't call. He was too busy blowing Roslyn's back out to be bothered with his supposed to be girlfriend.

"Don't thank me. I ain't make you fine!" he laughed. She began to laugh until the door bell began to chime.

"Who the heck is at our house this late?" she wondered and looked out of the window. She saw the strange car and went to check with her mother.

"Expecting company?" Mrs Worthington asked as she secured her robe while coming from her bedroom.

"No, are you?" Kelondra dared and smiled. She was hoping her mother would start dating again since her dad sure was.

"Is your brother home?" the mother asked and looked down the hall. A sinking feeling settled on her heart and she knew right then.

"No," she said since she remembered when he left. She followed her mother to the front door as the bell chimed again.

"Yes?" Mrs Worthington asked through the glass panels that laced the double doors.

"Police department," Johnson announced and held up his badge for proof. Mrs Worthington looked to Latisha to see if she had one too.

"Oh," Latisha said and pulled hers on a chain from under her shirt.

"Is my son dead?" the woman asked as she pulled the door open. Kelondra gasped at the idea that hadn't crossed her mind. Her hand fell to her side with Marquis still on the line.

"Mrs Worthington?" Johnson asked somewhere between stoic and callous.

"May we come in?" Latisha asked as she stepped in front of her partner. She may have hated giving death notifications but still did it better than her blunt partner.

"Yes," Mrs Worthington sighed and stepped aside.

"Is your son, Kenneth Worthington?" the lady cop asked once

they were seated in the living room. Kelondra's thigh was pressed against her mother's on the sofa.

"Yes. Is he dead?" the woman asked again. Anything less than that could be fixed.

"Yes. I'm sorry but he was the victim of a robbery and was shot," the woman explained.

"How?" the mother asked but she meant where. Things like that just didn't happen on this side of town which made things that much more confusing.

"Ashby street," Johnson answered since he wanted to say something. He tried to ignore the caramel calves revealed beneath the robe. It was either them or the round mounds of breast filling out her robe. They were enough to keep his eyes off the teen in tank top and shorts.

"Downtown? What in the world would he be doing on Ashby street?" the woman wondered and looked to her daughter. She could tell in an instant that the girl had the answer to that question if nothing else. Latisha caught the tacit exchange but didn't press. Not yet anyway.

"Can I see his room? While detective Johnson answers your questions" Latisha asked so she could get the girl alone.

"I'll show her," Kelondra offered and led the way. She took her up to her brother's bedroom and opened the door.

"What was he doing downtown?" the detective asked in a hush. Whispers get whispers so the girl matched her volume.

"Drugs. Kenneth and my boyfriend, ex boyfriend I mean. They sell weed. They get it from Atlanta," she answered.

"Where's your boyfriend now?" Latisha asked and pulled her pad to write it down. Kelondra finally remembered being on the line when she looked at her phone. "Is that him?"

"No," she replied and hung up. She called Carey's phone but it went straight to voicemail. "Carey Rollins. Do you need his number?"

"Sure," she agreed even though she doubted he had anything

to add since Kenneth arrived alone. It was obvious that Kenneth did know his killer so perhaps his friend would too.

"She didn't have any more questions," Johnson offered as an explanation for appearing at the bedroom door.

"Make sure your mom is OK. We'll just be a few minutes..." Latisha suggested and sent Kelondra on her way so they could search the room.

Johnson went straight for the walk-in closet while she hit the drawers. Mrs Worthington wasn't one of those mothers who searched rooms so Kenneth hadn't honed his hiding skills. Both cops hit payday rather quickly.

"Got cash!" Latisha declared as she pulled out a shoebox lined with money.

"Got dope!" he announced from the closet. He came out with a large bag of weed and scales. "Wanna log it?"

"Nah. What's the point," she said and tucked the box under her arm. He put the weed into a gym bag and followed her out.

"The coroner's office will be in contact tomorrow. So you can make arrangements," Latisha offered but didn't offer any of the cash she found. Her and her partner would split it and the weed as spoils of war.

MARQUIS WAS the first one to hear the tragic news but only shared it with his mother. Still by the time he awoke the news had traveled at the speed of the internet. His notifications were filled with people wanting to be first to spread the grim news. Kenneth 'Keto Cash's social media accounts were flooded with condolences. Yet his so-called best friend was the last one to get the news.

"Uh, uh. Un-huh, Un-huh!" Roslyn moaned as Carey humped her for breakfast. Her parents would be home in an hour so this was one for the road.

"Mmhm!" he agreed since the bare pussy felt better through the latex. They had run out of rubbers through the night so he had to stay diligent. Due diligence required closely monitoring the tingles pulsing through his body. He waited just until they reached the tip of his dick and snatched it out of her.

"That's right!" Roslyn comforted as she leaned up to watch him skeet on her belly.

"Shit!" he exclaimed and crumpled on top of her. She giggled in pride at her sexual prowess. This was a good time for another sexual selfie so she reached for her phone.

"Dang!" Roslyn giggled as the incoming notifications buzzed her phone for a full few minutes before she could use it. There were fifty messages, all saying the same thing. "Oh shit!"

"What?" Carey reeled since the stark terror in her tone meant something more serious than the latest celebrity couple's breakup.

"It's Keto, he's dead!" she informed and turned her screen. Carey refused to accept the news from her phone so he turned his back on. It too buzzed with the same notifications and bad news.

"Shit!" he shouted and scrambled out of her bed. He scrambled to get his clothes on and out of the house. A nosey neighbor shook her head as the half dressed black boy rushed from the house and hopped into his car. Most of the voicemails were from Kelondra but he didn't bother checking yet. Instead he just called her directly.

"Where have you been?" Kelondra asked when she took his call.

"Huh?" he asked since it sounded better than the answer. It bought enough time to come up with a better one than 'up in Roslyn's guts'. "Yeah, no, I was at home. Wasn't feeling well so I turned the phone off and got some rest. I'm on the way over there now!"

"Oh, OK," she said, sighed and hung up. Good timing since Carey's mom had popped on the line next.

"Hey mom," he answered.

"Oh my God! Are you OK? Where are you!" she demanded. The woman had been frantic since hearing the news since her son and the dead guy were two peas in a pod. One of those peas was now on a slab in the mall and the other hadn't come home all night.

"Yes, I'm fine mom. I wasn't with Kenneth last night. Spent a night at a friends. I'm on my way over to his house now," he explained.

"Ok. Good because Kelondra was just here looking for you," she said. Carey could only shake his head at the lie he had been caught in. He would just come up with another one by the time he got to the Worthington home.

Kelondra had spotted the lie as it formed on his tongue. Sorta like hurricane hunters do with a twister before it touches down. She didn't bother to call him on it since her brother was dead and that took precedence. Not to mention her heart wasn't in it anymore. Carey was now just a habit since he had been in her life for so long. Habits can be hard to break but Marquis could help with that.

After she buried her brother that is.

CHAPTER 11

"This bitch," Kelondra mumbled under her breath as Roslyn approached at the funeral.

"Kelondra!" Mrs Worthington reeled since she wasn't as far under her breath as she thought. She had never heard her darling daughter use such language but then again the girl never had to bury her brother before either.

"I'm so sorry! I loved..." the girl was trying to say before being rudely interrupted.

'Chu!' Kelondra interrupted the condolences by spitting directly in Roslyn's face. Her mouth had been open so some of the spit went in there as well.

"Kelondra!" he mother reeled again. She glanced around to make sure the scene didn't make a scene. Funerals were social events after all and she was a social creature. A blemish on the flawless send off would be just dreadful.

"She was busy fucking my boyfriend while Kenneth got killed," she hissed as the girl slinked away.

The police had returned Kenneth's phone after processing it for clues. It led them straight to a suspect since Scooter was the last one he spoke with. They ran Scooter's phone and the pings from cell phone towers put him right on the scene right on time. The hoodie and shades couldn't conceal that.

He was dumb enough to hold on to the same weapon when he was picked up. Not only did ballistics match but Kenneth's DNA was found on the gun from the blow back of the close range assassination attempt. Still, he was only charged with armed robbery and aggravated assault since he left the victim alive.

The GPS led straight to the car thieves since one one them parked it in his driveway like it was his. He didn't want to go down alone so he told on his friend before his fingerprints could. They both got knocked off and held on theft by taking charges.

Ray-ray and Bay-bay were arrested in the same parking lot of the same store where they committed the crime. Cousin or no cousin Bay-bay quickly threw Ray-ray under the bus since he was the shooter. That same bus ran him over too since he was charged with murder as well. It was all tied up in a neat little bow but that did little to soothe the grieving family.

"I'm sorry about your loss," detective Johnson offered and pulled the grieving mother into an awkward hug. It wasn't unusual for detectives to attend funerals from time to time. Latisha wasn't present because Mrs Worthington's impressions in her robe didn't leave the same impression on the woman.

"Um, OK. Thank you?" she replied and extracted herself from his clutches. They spoke from a respectful distance as Carey Rollins approached Kelondra.

"Carey?" Kelondra literally had to ask since he looked so different. She had seen his C-note persona often but it was totally inappropriate for a funeral.

"Yuh," he grunted like his favorite rapper always said. He was squeezed into a tight pair of skinny jeans and woman's blouse just like his favorite rapper wore. On his feet were a pair of large, gaudy, expensive tennis shoes. He rubbed his nostrils since the coke he just snorted with Roslyn still made it tingle.

"And..." she had to ask again since everyone else who came over had condolences.

"Shit fucked up," he shrugged. Kelondra blinked to see if he was serious. He was so she decided to get serious as well.

"No, what's fucked up is you fucking that thot, cheerleader reject, druggy!" she barked and turned her mother's head. Carey didn't respond so she continued without him. "I got my brother's phone. I saw your last text. And pics! Oh, and I went to your house to make sure you were OK but you weren't home. Get your lies straight!"

"Yuh," he shrugged again and looked down at his friend. Something had changed in him when his friend got murdered. A part of him had died along with him. His heart.

"The fuck?" Kelondra cussed when he turned and walked off. He didn't even walk the same as he used to. Mainly because it's hard to walk manly in those tight ass britches.

"The fuck is right!" her mother agreed as she saw her ex husband approaching. He looked a lot different too since the young girl on his arm made him feel younger himself.

"Hey there Madelyn. You remember Kendra," Mr Worthington introduced. If the time wasn't awkward enough the young woman tossed fuel on fire when she couldn't spare a second to look up from her phone.

"Hey," Kendra offered with a wiggle of her manicured fingers and kept right on scrolling.

"Of course I remember the little tramp you hired as a secretary even though she couldn't type," Mrs Worthington replied and got an eye roll.

"Watch it Madelyn! She is my wife now!" he fussed indignantly.

"Wife? She's a child!" the woman fussed as they seemed to lose track of their dead kid laying in the box with his arms folded over his chest. Kelondra and detective Johnson watched the back and volley like a tennis match.

"Ion cook, Ion clean, let me tell you how I got 'thi ring..." the newest Mrs Worthington rapped, laughed, shimmied and lolled out her tongue. That was enough for Madelyn.

"Bitch..." she snapped and lunged for the woman. She managed to grab a handful of weave before the cop grabbed her by the waist and pulled her away.

"Oh hell naw!" Kendra growled when her weave dislodged from her head. Now her husband had to hold her back.

"Really? While my brother is right there! Dead! Right there, dead!" Kelondra fussed. She managed to bring all parties back to their senses but not before officially making a scene.

"You have my card. Call me if you need anything," detective Johnson offered once the box was covered with dirt. The dead was buried so the living went back to live until someone threw dirt on their caskets.

"Sure," the woman dismissed. She was grateful he captured everyone who had a hand in her son's death and couldn't imagine what else he could do for her. He had turned and walked away before it dawned on her after watching Kendra shift her hips and sashay away. "Excuse me, detective..."

"Yes!" Johnson twirled and eagerly replied.

"There is one thing you can possibly do for me," she revealed when he returned.

"RIGHT THERE! RIGHT THERE!" Madelyn Worthington shouted as Johnson dragged his big Johnson in and out of her lonely vagina. Her box had been vacant even before the divorce since Mr Worthington preferred the new pussy to the old old pussy he had at home.

His loss though because this was some good older, not old

pussy. In fact it was brand new pussy to the detective. It was a lot better than the pussy he scrounged up on in the hood. Grieving mother's, aunties and even grannys provided a steady flow of vagina but this was some good, suburban pussy. So good and clean he had to eat it first.

Mrs Worthington showed her appreciation for his greedy tongue by busting a nut in his mouth. She came so hard the hotel room shook a little bit. The combination of being sexually couped up and his cyclone tongue action. She really appreciated when he produced the large, rock hard dick. It was bigger than her ex-husband's, which was a mental snub even if he would never know about it.

What was even more impressive was his rhythmic stroke. Almost slow dancing a slow drag in her vagina. He pushed, pulled, dipped and dragged it until she came to yet another quivering orgasm. He paused long enough for her to regain her composure, then started all over again.

"Right, here?" he asked as if he didn't know. Her scrunched up face announced the next orgasm before her body seized and shivered. "Guess so."

"Whew! I had no idea just how much I needed that!" Madelyn reeled once she recovered from this last orgasm. She hadn't come this many times in a month with her ex husband.

"Do you have to go?" Johnson asked, sounding disappointed when she rolled off the bed.

"Yes! I just buried my son and I left my daughter alone to get laid. I..." she was saying until he got up and she watched the Johnson swing between his legs. She sat back down and reached for her phone. "Maybe I can stay a little while longer..."

"Hello! Are you OK? Where are you?" Kelondra rattled as she took her mother's call. She had been worried since she abruptly left the funeral with the detective. She naturally assumed it pertained to her brother.

"Yeah, hey. I'm better than I've been in years!" Madelyn answered the first two questions and skipped the third.

"When are you coming home!" her daughter demanded.

"Oh, it could be a while..." she replied as Johnson's Johnson grew stiff in her hand. "Don't wait up!"

"Mother I..." Kelondra was saying until another voice replied.

"It's me," Marquis said since the call switched back to him when her mother hung up.

"I think my mom is getting..." she wondered, then shook it off. "Come get me!"

"I can't. I'm on my way," he answered twice. Marquita didn't usually let him take the car alone but he decided to try his luck. He found her at the computer desk instead of her bedroom. "What are you doing mama?"

"Studying!" she declared as if he should have known. "Shoot, them folks at my job making millions!"

"Oh," he replied since he really wasn't interested. He had his own interest in mind. "You ain't even gotta worry about none of that! One more year and I can get a name and likeness deal! That's at least a mil!"

"Your mil, mama wanna earn her own!" Marquita announced with new found enthusiasm. She was on a mission to outdo every one of those women who turned their noses up at her the first day. Even Deloris who was content to let her spend all day on tiktok since her son was a future star.

"That's what's up mama!" he cheered, genuinely impressed. But still, had a mission of his own. "Mama, can I use your car? Kelondra just buried her brother and..."

"Keys in my purse. I don't know why you ain't wanna go to the funeral," she replied and pointed to her bag.

"Nah, I cain't do no more of them," he sighed. The hood was just one long funeral and that shit gets old.

"I know baby. That's why I don't mind you using the car out here," she explained the difference that allowed him use of the vehicle on his own. It had nothing to do with him being the reason she was driving a new car either. "Them niggas just don't care. Rob anybody for anything."

"Thanks mama. I won't be long," he assured with a kiss on her cheek.

"Mmhm, just don't get nare one of these white gals pregnant!" she called after him. He was already out the door but she got it off her chest. "Ion know what it is with y'all black men and 'dese white women..."

Meanwhile Marquis made sure to buckle up and obey all traffic rules. He was still driving while black and that's a moving violation in lots of locales. This one too most of the time but the Williams family car and faces where shown to law enforcement to make sure the future star wasn't harassed.

"Sheesh," Marquis sighed as he pulled up into the driveway. Kenneth's car was parked in front of Kelondra's but it looked dead. It was filled with blunt clips, beer bottles and a few filled condoms since a Benz will pull a lot of pussy in the hood. He didn't realize he hadn't budged until the front door opened.

"Hey," Kelondra called and looked down the block for her mom. She was good though since her mom was busy looking back at detective Johnson delivering back shots.

"Hey," he agreed and followed her inside. "Nice house."

"Thanks," she shrugged and took his word for it. It may have been extra for him but was everyday, normal to her. So was having company in her bedroom so that's where she led him.

"Oh, ok?" Marquis said when he realized where they ended up. He sat on the edge of the bed and looked around. He took in the tasteful and expensive bedroom set before noticing the set of big thighs protruding from the tiny shorts.

"Excuse my appearance," she offered when she saw him scanning her from bare feet to messy bun.

"Naw, you look good shawty," he had to admit since in between the top and bottom was luscious lady lumps. The tiny shorts were pulled up snugly into her plump crotch, just below the flat stomach and firm breast. He shook it off and searched for some appropriate words for her time of grief. They usually say, 'long live so and so' in his old hood but that shit just sounded stupid. How is someone dead supposed to live long? His mind drifted to other odd sayings and quirks from the hood.

Kelondra was deep in thought as well. There was no more vacillating at this point, she just wasn't sure how to go about what she had in mind. She had been a good girl throughout her life and bad shit still happened. Her parents divorced, her brother was dead and her boyfriend cheated on her with the campus slut. She let out a sigh and jumped in with both feet.

"What are you doing!" Marquis shrieked and hopped to his feet when she lifted her shirt over her head. His shock didn't stop him from looking at the prettiest set of breasts he had ever seen.

"Getting undressed. It's what people do when they make love," she explained as she peeled off the shorts.

"Ye ain't gotta do this shawty," he said in his full hood vernacular that made her pussy jump. "I know you got a lot on yo mind, and..."

"Are you trying to talk me out of it?" she tilted her head and asked as she pulled her comforter back and climbed in her bed.

"Huh?" he asked since that wouldn't make much sense. He kicked off his tennis shoes and came around the other side of the bed. He had been fucking for years but somehow felt shy tonight. He sat on the bed and pulled his clothes off before sliding under the comforter with her. He expected her softness but her body was hotter than he ever felt before. "Damn shawty!"

"Is something wrong?" Kelondra pouted when she saw the grimace on his face.

"Naw," he replied and paused to kiss those full lips. "Err thing is just right!"

It sure felt right when they made out hot and heavy. Both reached for the other's genitals at the same time. She found him long and hard while she was soft and wet. Their tongues never left each other's mouth as they fondled and caressed. Soon the moment of truth came when he found himself on top and between her legs.

"Shit," Marquis fussed at the box of condoms he left in his drawer. He wasn't expecting sex so he didn't think to bring them.

"Is something wrong?" she asked again since this was all new to her.

"Everything is right," he said as he rubbed his erection against her slippery virginity. One push and the girl was a woman.

"Ouch," she complained once, then took it like a champ.

"You OK?" he asked and paused. He was prepared to stop if she wasn't but she was.

"Yes," she nodded and restarted his short strokes. He had enough dick to deliver long strokes but knew she wasn't ready for that. He knew she was a virgin from their frequent conversations and took it slow and easy.

Kelondra had a few things on her mind at the same time. Her face twisted at the incongruity of the pain and pleasure of the same act. The touch of a man made her tingle to her soul but that shit hurt at the same time. More importantly, she had done the deed. She could now add it to her life's resume. It was also payback for Carey's cheating even if he didn't know about it, Then, there was...

"Shit!" Marquis grunted and exploded inside the brand new box. He repeated himself when he thought about exploding in the brand new box. "Shit!"

"What's wrong?" Kelondra reeled when he suddenly snatched from her snatch.

"Huh? Oh, naw. Nothing," he replied and kissed those lips again. "But, we go together now."

"What about Carey?" she asked almost fearfully.

"Fuck Carey!" he said and took his woman just like he took his position on the team.

CHAPTER 12

"Talk to him!" Mrs Rollins demanded when Carey Junior's footsteps came down the stairs.

"Oh, ok," he sighed even though he really didn't want to. They had discussed the radical changes in their son over the last few weeks but he really didn't want to talk to him. Carey was rude and short whenever they had to interact.

Carey senior actually had more conversations with Miss Williams across the street than the people he took care of. He would masterbate while he watched her wash the car each Saturday, then make his way over. They talked about something different each time since she picked his brain for information on a variety of subjects.

Purely platonic and neither even flirted with the other. Which was new to Marquita who had plenty of dick without conversation. So having good conversations without dick was a refreshing change. Carey too was refreshed by the woman who didn't correct him or contradict him at every turn.

"Uh, son..." Carey offered gently so as not to set the increasingly volatile teen off. His mother had catered to his tantrums and hissy fits since he was a small child so it was no surprise he was entering adulthood with the same bad attitude.

"The fuck?" he snapped at his movement to the front door being impeded with talk. Didn't they see he was a whole hood nigga in his skinny jeans and big colorful shoes. And don't even worry about what was in the tote bag he toted everywhere he went.

"Nig..." the father began but the mother cut in.

"Coach called and said you quit the team?" Sinclair asked gingerly.

"Man fuck them folks!" he snapped and snarled.

"What the..." Mr Rollins wondered at the flash of gold in his mouth.

"Yeah, you see it! Young nigga got ten racks in his grill!" the teen barked and gave a grimace to show off his new grill. Business was booming since he didn't have a partner anymore. Plus he had moved up and on to slinging cocaine. That venture wasn't as profitable as the weed since he was inhaling lines everyday. "Don't hate cuz you lame!"

"Nigga, I'll..." the father finally snapped and stood.

"You want smoke?" Carey dared his dad but luckily his mother intervened.

"That's enough out of you!" she declared and held her husband back.

"Me?" Carey senior reeled in disbelief when he realized she was talking to him. Carey junior just walked out and went to handle his business.

"Yes you! You were too hard on him!" she fussed like it was his idea when he didn't even want to talk to him.

"I didn't even want to talk to the nigga!" he reminded.

"I can't with you when you're like this!" Sinclair huffed and stormed out.

"Good! Don't!" he said after her. He watched her pull away before Marquita came out with her bucket and rags. Carey slipped up to his favorite perch with his favorite lube and squeezed one off.

※

CAREY FELT like a hood star as he headed downtown to the hood. The music was booming, weed billowing and white girl bobbing below with a mouthful of dick. Roslyn paused the blow job to take a hit of coke up each nostril, then back to the dick.

"Shit!" he shouted and filled her mouth just like she just filled her nose. He held the steering wheel tightly so he wouldn't swerve.

"Gimme that!" Roslyn giggled giddily when she came up and took the blunt from his lips.

"You can go on and rock out with that," he chuckled since she did just swallow a bunch of babies. The expensive car turned heads once again when they wove through the city streets.

Man-man was already looking out his window when they pulled into his apartments. He was the man around here which gave Carey a pass to come and go, but this was the hood and niggas were hungry. Down right famished and he was looking like something to eat. One false move and Man-man could get it too. They say there's no honor amongst thieves but hood niggas ain't shit.

"Naw nigga," Man-man told a pack of teens eyeing his food. He was still overcharging Carey for weed and now the coke.

"Sup my guy!" Carey greeted as he and Roslyn entered the apartment.

"That nigga C-note!" Man-man said with the little laugh that always came along with it. He knew he was a nerdy rich kid from the burbs and couldn't take him seriously. Carey knew it too but it stung a little more in front of his girl.

"Yeah," he said like a dare and cocked his head. They never

spoke about the fact that Scooter set up the robbery that got his friend killed. After all, that was personal. This was business.

"You the man!" he laughed again and raised his hands in mock surrender.

"A'ight," C-note said and began removing cash from the bag.

"So, who is your friend? You tryna sell her?" Man-man asked since dudes sold white girls all the time.

"Nah nigga, this my bitch!" he snapped just like his favorite rapper said in his latest song.

"Easy killer!" Man-man said with that same humorless, condescending chuckle. "You guys wanna hang out? Party a little bit?"

"No! Yes!" C-note and Roslyn both shot back with the same enthusiasm.

"Can we stay for a little while?" Roslyn pleaded. Literally begged with her hands together like it was prayer. He only brought her to show off his hood connection but she knew hood from plywood. Man-man was the real deal and that excited her.

"Hell yeah!" Man-man answered for him and patted the sofa next to him.

"I got business," C-note said and shrugged. He had money to make plus plenty of other hoes back in the burbs. If she wanted to stay with a belly full of his babies it was cool with him.

Roslyn had a mouth full of hood dick before C-note made it out the complex.

"THERE'S C-NOTE!" Big Dog cheered when Carey walked into the gym on game night. He looked more like he was about to perform a rap concert than playing a basketball game.

"Is he playing?" Tank wanted to know. They were playing the team that destroyed them last season. The whole team desperately wanted to return the favor. C-note could be a prick but did have a nice jumper.

"I just wanna know where my sister is?" Roslyn's brother wanted to know. He was the first one to make it over to him. "Where's Roslyn?"

"Don't know. Don't care," he shrugged and walked by the rest of the team as if he didn't even see them. He took a seat with some more good girls on the edge and leaned back.

"Fuck boy," Marquis snarled at him. Some topless pictures of Kelondra had been circulating and they could only have come from him. She urged him to leave it alone since most pictures of most girls were far worse than that. Roslyn had several videos and pictures in rotation. She would have plenty more since she was being passed around the hood right then.

"Look!" Hannah told Kelondra when she spotted Carey and the girls.

"No thanks," she huffed since she had already seen him. Seeing him once was enough so she didn't need or want to see him again.

Carey kept his eye on Kelondra to see if she wanted him back. She hadn't taken or returned any of his calls, text, DMs or smoke signals. Leaking the topless photo was the smoke signal to get her to realize she needed him. Especially since he had a few pics of that pretty vagina she was blessed with.

The only time his eyes left the cheerleaders was when the crowd reacted to the happenings on the court. Which turned out to be every few seconds since Marquis Williams went crazy. The home crowd thundered every time he hit a three, made a steal or a vicious dunk.

"Fucking sellout!" Carey barked towards his father when he saw him clapping and cheering on his rival. He happened to be sitting next to Marquis's mother instead of his own. Mrs Rollins opted out of coming since her son was no longer on the team.

The neighbors gravitated next to each other to cheer on the home team.

This was the defending state champs so college and NBA scouts were in attendance. Last season's game was a blowout but this game was close. Marquis and the opposing team went back and forth, bucket for bucket. Even double teams couldn't stop the kid who made his whole team better. In the end it was a buzzer beater from the corner that sealed the deal. The team mobbed Marquis but the cheerleaders got to him first.

"Great game baby!" Kelondra cheered and jumped into his arms. Speculations were confirmed when they shared a passionate kiss right there on the spot.

"Arhgh!" Carey gasped and grabbed his chest like Fred G Sanford. His heart broke so hard it forced a sound from his mouth. The girls looked at him, then each other as he stormed from the gym.

Carey marched out to the parking lot and hit his key fob. He reached into his car and grabbed the bag containing the ghost gun. He remembered the coke and took a healthy hit up each nostril. Now he was set to shoot up his school. Especially Marquis for taking more than just his girl. It was like he took his whole life. He marched back towards the gymnasium with murder on his mind.

"Fuck!" Carey screamed at the top of his lungs when he realized he was no killer. He wasn't even C-note, he was just a chump. A call stole his attention so he got in the car and pulled away. The happy people inside had no idea how close they came to a massacre. He didn't know the number so he answered with a question. "Hello?"

"Come get me," a raspy voice asked.

"Roslyn?" he asked since he wasn't sure. Her throat was extremely sore and raw after a week in the hood.

"Yes. Come, get me. Please," she pleaded.

"I'm on the way!" he said and pulled away from what was almost a crime scene. "Where are you?"

"Um, Atlanta?" was all she knew. She looked around and read the street signs. "North avenue."

"Fuck!" Carey grunted when he realized she was in a particularly notorious section of the city known as the Bluff. The gun on his lap reassured him that everything would be alright. Guns can make things alright, but there were plenty guns in the Bluff.

Roslyn stayed on the phone with Carey as he sped down from the suburbs. He could hear a variety of men push up on her as she waited. A white girl on a payphone on this side of town had 'rental pussy' all over her. She had declined a long line of drugs, cash and pick up lines when Carey came barreling into the parking lot. Sooner or later someone was going to throw her over his shoulder like a sack of wheat and take her.

The way he rolled up made the thugs think it was the police so they spread out a little. A little was all Roslyn needed to get into the car. He sped off as the jackers rushed towards him to rob him. The ghost gun whispered 'shoot them', from his waist but Carey was no killer. Plus, he had what he came for.

"Thank you," Roslyn moaned and leaned her head on her shoulder. She looked tired, with dark bags under her eyes. Her lips were chapped from all the miles put on them over the last week. A good dose of penicillin would clear up the clap she picked up. The handprints on her ass would dissipate. It was the emotional scars from her ordeal that would take longer to heal.

"You're welcome. You're safe," he replied and felt good about it. "You want some coke? Some smoke?"

"No!" she reeled from just the mention of drugs.

"What did they do to you?" he had to ask. The look of sheer terror on her face demanded he did.

"What didn't they do to me," she sighed. She had told herself she would keep it to herself but it was too heavy to carry alone. "I was at Man-man's apartment for a couple days. We partied, got high, had sex. Then he let his friend fuck me. Then another and another. Two days ago I woke up and some dude claimed he bought me and carried me away. Two more days with him until he passed me around to his friends. Finally I got away and called you."

"And I came running," Carey said, feeling proud of himself. That's the thing about doing good, it makes you feel good.

"You did," she said and leaned back on his shoulder while he drove. "I would suck your cock but I think my jaw is unhinged."

"I bet," he sighed and drove her home.

CHAPTER 13

"Sup shawty. You tryna holla at me?" Man-man asked when he took the call from C-note.

"Hell yeah! And I'ma need err thang you got!" he shot back.

"Shit I'm sitting pretty right now! Just re-upped from the *connect!*" the dope boy bragged. If he could sell it all to Carey at triple the price he would be winning.

"I want it all. Weed, coke, pills if you got 'em," he said as he sped towards the hood. Carey rarely ventured into the hood after dark since even he knew he really wasn't built like that. He had recently sold out on everything and there was money to be made. The usual faces in the apartments had been replaced by the night crew. They all watched the expensive vehicle carefully as it pulled in.

"Come on!" Man-man called from the groove in the sofa.

"Sup my nigga?" C-note greeted with the inflection of a question.

"You my nigga," he laughed that dry laugh he usually laughed at the nerdy kid. He had trouble taking him seriously since he was seriously overcharging him. Keto found out the hard way about doing business in the hood. Sure there were better prices but chances of getting robbed and killed dramatically increased as well. "Bruh, you see that game the other night? My nigga Marquis Williams went ham out there! Dropped forty six on they hoe asses!"

"You know him? Like, personally?" C-note asked and titled his head.

"Hell yeah! He really is from around here! He just moved out there a lil while ago," he explained.

"That's me?" C-note asked of the stacks of drugs on the small dinette table.

"Hells yeah! That's me?" Man-man asked and nodded to the bag that looked like it had enough bread to cover the fee.

"Hells yeah," he repeated and dug into the bag. "Got something from Roslyn for you too!"

"That bitch had some fiyah ass head!" he laughed until the barrel of the gun came into focus. "Nigga, I know your soft ass ain't finna try to rob me!"

"Ain't no finna to it. Just like y'all did my partner Keto," C-note growled. He followed the dope boy's eyes over to the AK/47 leaning against the wall. White people prefered the AR/15 to shoot up shit while the hood niggas still relied on the Automatic Kalashnikov designed in 1947. It's been putting people in the dirt for seventy five years now.

"You got that," Man-man conceded. He couldn't make it to the weapon before the kid put nine slugs in his back. He would let him take the drugs and gun him down from the window.

"I know I got that! I took it. Tell Keto I said hey," Carey said and tugged on the trigger. He didn't do bad for his first time firing a gun. He had aimed at his face but the bullet tore into his neck. It would be just as fatal, just slower.

C-note curiously cocked his head and moved closer as Man-man struggled to keep his blood inside of his body. His mouth moved with words that wouldn't come since his vocal cords were shredded by the bullet. Another bullet to his head would have been merciful but C-note wasn't feeling very merciful. After all, no one showed Keto any mercy when he was robbed three times in five minutes. No one showed Roslyn's tonsils or vagina any mercy as she was passed around for a week.

"I think you better let it go..." C-note sang in his best Teddy Pendergrass voice. Man-man just squeezed his neck with all he had but the blood still seeped and leaked until more of it was on him than in him. His body went limp when he finally did let it go. "Looks like another love TKO..."

THE LINES between Carey Rollins junior and C-note had been blurred for years. Now that C-note was a killer he all but killed off his alter ego. He didn't need Carey much anymore so he stayed hidden. Even around the house it was C-note who now roamed.

Carey senior disliked the boy more and more so he avoided him like the plague. Even his mother wasn't sure what to make of this next chapter in their lives. She could only hope it too would fizzle out. They had survived his cowboy phase, the boy scouts, tennis, football and basketball. The school year was almost over and he would be off to college.

It's been said that the best way to get over a bitch was to get on the next bitch and that's exactly what C-note did. He ran through as many of his classmates as he could. A task made easier since plenty of the girls were jealous of Kelondra so fucking her ex made them feel on her level. Even if her next was so much better than her ex. By far his favorite was Kelondra's ex best friend Katie.

"Your son is at it again!" Carey senior fussed when sounds of sex drifted down the hall.

"He's going through a rough spot," Sinclair suggested on his behalf. She always had an excuse for the boy even when being as disrespectful as fucking in the house while they were home.

"Doesn't sound too rough to me," the father said as Katie's moans reached them as she reached her peak.

"I'm coming!" Katie shrieked as C-note pounded away. She did, then he did and the noise came to an end.

"At least someone is getting some in this house," he mumbled loud enough to be heard.

"See! That's why I can't with you!" Mrs Rollins fussed and grabbed her purse.

"See ya!" he laughed since that was exactly what he knew she would do. It was almost car wash time so he peeked out the window to see if the neighbor had gotten started. She hadn't so he went for a glass of juice.

"Hey Mr Rollins!" Katie sang in her bubbly, white girl way.

"Um, hey there," he replied and blushed at the big white breast hanging out of her bikini top.

"You wanna hit my nigga?" C-note asked his dad. His father just blinked as he processed the words. He would love some pussy but was unhappily married to his mother. Even Katie looked on, waiting for an answer. "I won't tell mom."

"Nothing to tell. Now take your friend home," he said sternly and walked back to his room.

"Ole hating ass nigga," C-note mumbled at his back. Carey heard him but decided against checking him on it. He'd much rather bust his weekly nut and go talk to Marquita afterwards.

"Are you going to the party tonight?" Katie asked and quickly regretted it. The rich kids partied every weekend but this weekend was the basketball teams party for winning the division. The big celebration before moving on to the state championship tournament. "My bad."

"It's all good. Of course I'ma be there!" he cheered with a wicked grin. Not only did he have plenty customers there he also knew Kelondra and Marquis would be there. Their relationship had been public since sharing a kiss at the game. Now they made out in the halls like all the other couples. Now he had Katie to throw up in Kelondra's face. "Wouldn't miss it for the world!"

❦

"YOUR EX IS GOING to be at the party you know," Kelondra teased as Marquis drove her car to the party. Marquita offered him her car but it was just a car. Kelondra drove a Benz.

"My who?" he laughed since the only ex he knew of Bombquisha back in the hood.

"Katie," she specified. She heard he tricked off with a few girls at school before they hooked up but Katie was the only one she had been really cool with. Now that the latest fad seemed to be fucking her ex she wanted to make sure he was secured.

"Man, I just wanted some white girl head! Everybody in the hood was always talking about some white girl head! They say it's magical!" he laughed at his own joke.

"Well, black girls have magic too," she quipped as they reached the party house for the night.

"I like magic?" he asked as she got out. They had sex a few times but she had yet to show him her real super powers.

"I bet you do," she said and put some sway in her hips for him. "Play your cards right and I just might make your dick disappear, down my throat."

"Deal them then!" he laughed. The party was in full swing when they arrived since white people didn't do colored people's time. They did dance funny though so they paused to watch the awkward jerking movements on the makeshift dance floor.

"Marquis!" a team member called and waved him over.

"Go ahead. I'll be with my squad," Kelondra said since the cheerleader squad was in attendance. They shared a quick kiss before going their separate ways.

"Hope her mouth tastes like my dick," C-note snarled when he watched the kiss from his seat. He was posted up with a bunch of young addicts. Smoking, drinking and snorting while playing in some chick's vagina. He got drunker and higher as the night marched on.

C-note alternated between watching his old team and old girlfriend. Then zoomed in on the common denominator for losing them both. Marquis flashed his million dollar smile as he interacted with the team. A couple times when he looked over a Kelondra she was looking over at Marquis.

"Bitch all in love," he growled. He thought about starting some shit but had left the gun in his car.

"That's fucked up dude. First he takes your position, then takes your bitch! Bet he's putting her in all kinds of positions!" Kyle said in a drunken slur and laughed.

"Chill Kyle," Chad urged. He personally was afraid of this C-note guy. He grew up with Carey and didn't recognize him anymore.

"I should go knock his ass out?" C-note asked. Instigators all raised their hands like at an auction, bidding on an item.

"Fold his ass up like we used to on the wrestling team!" another added. Marquis was in the middle of laughing at someone's joke when his head turned and made accidental eye contact with C-note.

"Oh, this nigga just tried me!" C-note barked and stood.

"Uh oh," Big Dog said when he saw C-note leading the pack of stoners their way. He actually stepped forward to be a barrier between him and Marquis.

"Shoot!" Kelondra fussed when she saw the impending drama about to unfold.

"Step aside. Let him get it off his chest," Marquis insisted when his nemesis arrived. "Sup neighbor. Err thing good?"

"Hell naw it ain't good! I heard you been poppin shit!" C-note said like the boys in the hood say. Except he was talking to a real boy from the hood.

"No you didn't but if you wanna hit, we can hit," Marquis said as Kelondra arrived. Both combatants had lifted their fist to do the dance that leads to a fight.

"Stop! Just stop!" she demanded as she stepped between the two.

"Move bitch!" C-note shouted and shoved her to the ground. He stepped over her as Marquis bent over to help her up. He was a sucker so he threw a sucker punch. Marquis dipped the sucker punch and scooped C-note into the air. Time seemed to pause for a moment when he reached the apex. Then resumed to real time when he slammed him down on his head.

"You got knocked the fuck out!" a kid teased but C-note couldn't hear it over his own snores.

"Are you OK?" Marquis asked as he helped Kelondra to her feet.

"Better than he is!" she snapped and tried to give C-note a kick. Luckily Marquis had a sense of honor that didn't allow kicking people while they were down.

"Un-uh, come on," he said and lifted her over the sleeping teen. The fight knocked the life out of the party just like C-note sleeping on the ground. People retreated to their cars and went their separate ways. Marquis was driving but it was Kelondra who picked him up, so he drove to his house. The trip was made in silence from the shock of the incident

"I can't believe him!" she fussed when they reached his driveway.

"Yeah, that's some sucker shit," Marquis agreed. Something dawned on him that put that pretty smile on his face. "I just played the cards he dealt..."

"You did!" she cackled at the joke, then got serious. She reached for his zipper and asked, "Wanna see a magic trick?"

"I do, I really do!" he cheered and got an instant erection as she removed his dick. He closed his eyes as the hot moisture of her mouth engulfed him. Those eyes popped back open when he felt her tonsils on the tip of his dick.

'Gawk, gawk, gawk' echoed through the car as she displayed her black girl magic.

"Fuck!" he moaned and squirmed in his seat. Come to find out white girl head had nothing on black girl head. Or Asian, African or Eskimo head.

"Mmhm!" Kelondra hummed when his feet shifted involuntarily underneath him. She clamped down and took a blast of babies right to her esophagus.

"Uh-oh," Marquis said when he heard a tap on the driver's side window. He looked up and tried to bring the object into focus. It almost registered before a brilliant flash took his life away.

It took Kelondra a few seconds to process the sound, the glass and the warm spray of blood that doused her face. She looked up and saw the smoking gun, then C-note's face behind it. There was a brief moment of extreme danger as he decided if she should live or die with her boyfriend. The porch light came on before he could decide so he walked back across the street and went home.

CHAPTER 14

"*B*aby?" Marquita asked as she answered the first gun shot she had heard since moving. She was almost relieved to see Kelondra leap from the vehicle covered in blood. It would be fine if it were her blood, she didn't mind. But her son wasn't moving. "Baby?"

"He, he, he shot him!" she screamed and pointed across the street. Carey had gone inside and into the shower.

"Who?" Marquita asked as she dialed 9-11. A call she realized was futile when she neared the car. She had seen enough dead bodies in her life to know one when she saw one. This one was her son. "Man, they done 'kilt my baby."

"What's going on? What happened? Who's shooting?" the neighbors asked as the gunshot brought them out in their robes. Most of the homeowners had pistols in their pockets to protect their families.

"What does that hoochie mama, hood rat have going on now!" Sinclair Rollins fussed as she and her husband went to investigate. Neither noticed that their son didn't join them as they stepped outside.

"It's Marquita!" Mr Rollins said with an urgency that made his wife squint at his back as he rushed over.

"What happened?" he asked Kelondra but she was too distraught to speak. He looked past her to Marquita cradling her dead son in her arms. Marquis had slumped out of the car when she opened the door so she sat on the concrete with the bloody corpse.

"They shot my baby. We moved all the way out here so no one would shoot him, and they shot him anyway," she said in a stoic disbelief.

"Who? Who shot him?" he asked her, then Kelondra as the first of what would be many police cars whipped up to a screeching stop. An ambulance was a few seconds behind it.

"Carey, it was Carey," Kelondra said in a whisper before the officer cleared the scene of spectators. He set up a perimeter so they would have to gawk from behind the police tape.

"He's gone," the paramedic declared at first sight. Not just because of the hole in his head but only dead people can stare off into nothing like that. A quick check of his pulse made it official. The medical examiner would use this as the time of death.

"Let's move these people out of my crime scene!" detective Graves ordered when he arrived. The crowd was already behind the police tape, he just liked to bark orders. They didn't get many homicides out here in West View so he was slightly giddy.

He was hoping for a real 'whodunit' so he could figure out who did it and claim the fame. The last murder in his jurisdiction was a run of the mill domestic violence. Mr killed Mrs so he could run off with a mistress. It took a half hour to solve that one.

"What do we got?" he asked, looking down at the dead body.

"Marquis Williams. Black male. Seventeen years old. One GSW to the face," the medical examiner reported.

"Witnesses?" he asked and looked over at Marquita and Kelondra huddled on the porch.

"The girlfriend was in the passenger seat. Mother heard the shot and came out," the cop spoke up.

"Take them both to headquarters. Separate cars, separate rooms," he said and went back to his detective stuff. All the while the killer watched from his bedroom window.

"I knew they would be trouble," Sinclair hissed as the body was bagged and taken away.

"Her son got killed and they are trouble?" Carey senior said, shaking his head and walking away. His son still hadn't come back out while the rest of the block had. Something was wrong and he was determined to find out what.

"THE MOTHER IS in room A. The girlfriend is in D. Her mother is in with her," a cop advised when the detective arrived back at the scene. He had taken the illegal liberty of looking around the victims house and room but there was nothing to find.

"I'll start with the girlfriend," he said to himself and headed to room D."Hello ladies, I'm sorry about all this,"

"Hello," Ms Worthington replied on behalf of her and her traumatized daughter. Streaks of smeared blood were visible on the girl's face but tears had carved a path down to her chin.

"Can you tell me what happened?" he asked softly and looked up to make sure the red light was lit on the camera.

"We were in the car and a shot went off and he was standing there with the gun!" Kelondra blurted.

"Let's take it slow. How long were you in the driveway? What were you guys doing? Did you argue?" he asked to get answers for questions that could come up in a court of law.

"Not long. We were just..." she said and paused to look sheepishly at her mother. She wasn't ready to give a blow by blow of the blow job so she decided, "We were making out. Kissing."

"I see," he nodded since he took note of the victim's penis being out of his pants. "Then what happened?"

"There was a knock on the window. Then the gunshot. I lifted my head and saw him with the gun," she explained, explaining more than she intended since she admitted her head was down. Her mother blushed while the detective got excited.

"Saw who with the gun?" he asked, ready to close his case.

"Carey. Carey Rollins. He is my, was my boyfriend. My ex boyfriend," she revealed. The revelation received a loud gasp from her mother. Kelondra backed up to the lopsided fight at the party and caught back up to the murder.

"Did you actually see him shoot the gun?" he needed to know since it would be an issue at trial.

"Well, no?" she admitted and began to cry again.

"One sec...." Detective Graves paused and stepped out into the hallway. He waved the captain over and requested a warrant. "Carey Rollins, malice murder, aggravated assault, possession of a firearm during the commission of a crime..."

"Can we go now? You know we recently buried her twin brother," Ms Worthington reminded when he returned. Not only was it true it was a good excuse to leave.

"Sure. Once again I'm sorry for your loss. Losses," he corrected and held the door. "I'll be in touch if we have any further questions."

The detective compared the mother and daughter's back sides as they left the room. He hadn't gotten a very good look at Marquita but knew her sizes from the brief search of her house. He even looked through her hamper for weapons but found none. After a few sips of his cold coffee he went in to talk to the grieving mother.

"Mrs Williams, I'm detective Graves. I'm sorry for your loss," he said as Marquita slumped in her seat.

"That weird boy across the street did this, didn't he? I bet it was him," she replied. She technically should have been in the hospital due to her state of shock.

"Who?" he asked to see if he came up with the same name.

"Carey," she quickly remembered but mainly because it was his father's name as well.

"Did Carey and Marquis have a fight about something?" he asked even though he knew. He just wondered if she knew. The world was finding out as they spoke since the fight was captured on several phones. Several of those videos were already uploaded.

"My son took his position on the basketball team!" she spat hotly. She determined that was the reason for her son's death. "A damn position!"

§

"OH MY GOD!" Carey senior reeled and wheeled away from his computer. He leaned forward and slammed the laptop shut as if that would make it go away. It wouldn't since the Ring cam footage was forever like herpes.

His curiosity led him to check the footage and he got more than he bargained for. He could very clearly see when Kelondra's car pulled into the driveway. The car had been parked in his own driveway enough to know it when he saw it.

His curiosity led him to speculate what was happening in the parked car when no one got out. He allowed his mind to wander to back when he and his now Mrs were courting. He would have been leaned back with his dick out, while she attempted to suck a husband out of it. Once she did she rarely sucked it since.

The reminiscing was interrupted when he saw his son pull into the driveway. He could so clearly see when Carey junior pulled a gun from his waistband and walked across the street.

There was no mistaking when he tapped on the window with the barrel. The Ring cam picked up both the flash and bang when he fired the gun.

Now Carey wasn't sure what scared him most. Witnessing his son commit a murder or the smug smirk he wore as he casually came home and went inside. The thought crossed his mind to delete the footage even though it would still be available on the company servers. A loud knock on the door stole him from that train of thought.

"Carey!" the police are at the door!" Mrs Rollins screeched at the top of her lungs.

"Already?" he wondered as he went to investigate. The police were no longer at the door since they were piling inside with guns drawn.

"Warrant! Hands up! On the ground!" the cops screamed as they barged in. It was incongruent commands like that that got people killed.

"Down!" Mr Rollins directed and pulled his wife to the hardwood floors.

"The fuck going on down here!" C-note barked as he came down the stairs.

"Show me your hands!" a cop screamed while red laser sights danced on his shirtless torso.

"For god sake show your hands and get down!" his father pleaded.

"Fuck twelve!" he shouted just like his favorite rapper always did. The cops tensed and slowly applied pressure to their triggers. Carey junior was about to die in the living room but his mother had other plans.

"Nooooo!" she screamed and leapt from
to her feet. She crossed the room in record speed and tackled her son to the floor. The cops jumped on his back and cuffed his hands behind his back. Now his mother wanted to know, "What is this about? Why are you arresting my son!"

"Murder," a cop announced and handed her the warrant. It included a search of the residence which meant, "We need you step outside please.

"My son didn't kill anyone! What's wrong with you people!" she fussed as her husband led her outside. Carey was still being placed in the back of a patrol car. "Don't say anything! We'll get you a lawyer honey!"

"OK mother," he replied like the gentle boy she once knew. Those steel cuffs have that effect when they get clamped tightly on the wrist. Had she not said that they would have tricked a full confession out of him.

"I'll call Duane," Mr Rollins nodded when deciding on a friend from college who had a criminal defense firm.

"This is all her fault. None of this would have happened if those hood people hadn't moved in!" Sinclair growled as Marquita got out of the police car that drove her home.

"No..." Carey senior began but couldn't bring himself to reveal what he saw on the Ring cam. Not that his wife was listening anyway since she was marching across the street to confront the grieving mother.

"My son is in jail because of you people!" she fussed as the woman tried to go inside. Marquita's mind was busy trying to figure out which substance or combination of substances in the house could put her out of this misery. She was ready to join her son at the morgue because life lost its meaning. The bright and beautiful future her son worked for had been violently snuffed out.

"Excuse me?" Marquita asked. She heard the words just fine but couldn't make sense of them. Her mind tried to move them around like the Soul Train word scramble but they didn't register.

"This is all your fault!" she repeated and slapped the woman in the face. It may have been Sinclair's first slap but Marquita was from Southwest Atl. She had been slapping hoes and taking slaps her whole life. Mr Rollins was just a few feet away but too far to prevent the sudden flurry of fist, fingernails, elbows and knees. He was too stunned to stop it, plus he kinda liked it. Lord knows he wanted to whoop her ass a few times over the years.

"Hey, stop, no, don't do that," he offered half-heartedly but didn't move to stop it. Luckily one of the cops rushed across the street and peeled Marquita off of Sinclair.

"Would you like to press charges ma'am?" the officer asked.

"Yes! I want her arrested!" Sinclair demanded through her bloody, puffed up lips.

"Uh, I was talking to her," the cop corrected and looked at Marquita.

"Naw, I just want to go to sleep," she sighed and went inside to cry herself to sleep.

CHAPTER 15

"Anything?" detective Graves asked when he arrived at the Rollins home. He didn't even acknowledge the homeowners sitting on the curb before entering their half a million dollar home.

"Everything!" one of the CSI techs announced happily. He held up a plastic bag containing a pistol. "It's most likely the murder weapon. It's been very recently fired. Damn near still warm!"

"Ghost gun?" Graves detected it when he didn't see any manufacturer name or serial numbers.

"Another one!" he said and shook his head. These dangerous and unregulated guns were popping up at more and more crime scenes. The 3D printed gun parts were sold on the internet and black markets. Easily assembled and untraceable.

"Got drugs too!" another cop said as he produced bags of weed and coke.

"And cash. Looks like our boy is a dope boy!" yet another officer announced when he produced stacks of dope boy cash.

"Drug related?" Graves suggested to himself. He needed an

explanation as to why a good kid from a good home, with good parents would suddenly become a killer. "Cameras?"

"Lots!" the tech replied and expounded. "Ring cameras up and down the block, including here."

"Let's take a look," the detective said, looking at the laptop on the desk. The tech rushed forward and made quick work of the password protection.

"Looks like someone likes 'Big booty hoochies', a lot!" the man laughed at the site in the history. "Hmp?"

"What?" Graves asked and looked over his shoulder for a glance of some big booty hoochies, because who really doesn't like big booty hoochies.

"He just reviewed the Ring footage..." he replied and pulled it up. Both were astonished at the brutal murder caught on camera.

"He didn't delete it! I wonder why he wouldn't delete it?" the cop asked to himself.

"Probably knew we would find it anyway. Didn't want to tamper with evidence?" he suggested correctly. Both made sense especially since a few more cameras caught pieces of evidence in the crime.

"Well, let's go see what young mister Rollins has to say for himself," Detective Graves said once they wrapped up searching the house. He knew the suspect would be shivering in an ice cold interrogation room. He just hoped he could get to him before he lawyered up.

"CAREY ROLLINS! GOOD TO SEE YOU!" Duane McCoy greeted his old college buddy. Like lots of college buddies they hadn't seen each other much since graduation.

"I wish under better circumstances," Carey sighed as they embraced. Duane and Sinclair shared a nod while the men hugged. They didn't like each other in college much since they both vied for Carey's attention. In the end the woman won since she had a vagina. Which is why a best friend with a vagina is a man's best bet.

"What's going on?" Duane needed to know. He answered the summons immediately but had no idea why he was here.

"They're trying to say Carey junior killed that boy!" Sinclair huffed.

"Little Carey?" the lawyer reeled incredibly. Carey junior was a little boy the last time he saw him at his own daughter's birthday party. He remembered his daughter beating him up so no way was this kid a murderer.

"Well, he's not so little anymore," Carey said as the Ring footage played in his mind. The flash of the gun made him wince again at the thought.

"Has he made a statement yet?" Duane pleaded. He knew if he did there would be no saving him. One time he walked into an interrogation room and saw the empty chicken box and grease on his client's mouth. He turned around and walked right back out without saying a word.

"No. I don't think he's been interviewed yet..." Carey said to his back as he rushed away.

"Duane McCoy. I represent Carey Rollins junior. I need to speak with my client!" he barked at the desk officer.

"Room three," he advised and led the way. The officer opened the door and stepped aside.

"Carey? I'm a friend of your dad. I'll be representing you," the layer said as he entered the room with his client. "Just let me do all the talking."

"O,o,o, ok," Carey stuttered. The cold steel feel of the cuffs explained he wasn't really about this life. The freezing room was an exclamation point.

"What happened to your head?" the observant attorney asked of the lump on his head.

"I got dumped on my head," Carey sighed. The videos were already going viral in the burbs and it looked worse than it was. That's a lot because it was pretty bad.

"Real quick, I need to know what happened," he whispered so his client could whisper back. He leaned in just in case the camera was recording even though the red light wasn't on. The trick gleaned information that couldn't be used in court but was still helpful in building a case.

"He um, slammed me on my head. At a party," Carey began with his excuse. It would be as far as he got for the moment since the door opened and in walked the homicide detective.

"Who are you?" Graves asked even though he couldn't be anyone other than a lawyer. Carey was eighteen so he didn't need a parent present to be interviewed.

"Duane McCoy, attorney at law," he said and extended his business card.

"Un-huh," he replied and ignored the card. He opened his laptop and pulled up what he wanted to show. He pressed play and spun it around.

"What are we supposed to be looking at?" the lawyer asked, ready to dispute whatever he said. Graves just nodded at the laptop since it said all that needed to be said.

"That's not me!" Carey whined as C-note fired the shot into the car. He wasn't disputing that it happened, just distinguishing himself from his alter ego.

"Sure doesn't look like my client!" McCoy laughed. The laughter died in his throat as the shooter came closer and closer until Carey's smiling face could clearly be seen.

"So, we just need to know why? You guys weren't fighting over a girl were you? I heard he took your spot on the court?" Graves asked. Luckily the lawyer was present because the spoiled brat was on the verge of a tantrum.

"My client needs medical attention asap! He has a visible contusion. Possibly a concussion!" the lawyer lawyered and wiggled his eyes at his client. It took Carey a second to catch on but he did.

"I feel dizzy..." he moaned right before falling out of the chair. Now the cops had no choice but to suspend the interview and get him to a hospital.

§♣

"WHAT ARE YOU LOOKING AT!" Sinclair demanded when she snuck up on her husband peering out of the window. It was the same window he made love to the neighbor in his mind with his dick in his hand. He was looking for a glimpse of Marquita but wouldn't tell her that. Good timing meant he didn't have to.

"Duane. He's pulling up now," he said as she pushed past to see for herself.

"Mmhm," she hummed and rubbed the knot on her head while looking at the house to the woman who gave it to her. Last night had been so hectic that she didn't even register the pain of getting her ass whooped until the morning.

"What's the word?" Carey asked as he opened the door for his friend. Paternal instinct wanted the best for his namesake, offspring but at the same time it shivered his soul to watch the murder. To know the hateful teen had a gun in their home shook him to his core.

"Can he come home!" Sinclair demanded as if her husband wasn't there. Carey junior may have been a monster but he was her little monster.

"No, he won't be coming home just yet," he informed. "He'll be discharged from the hospital today and taken to jail."

"What about a bond? Can you get him out on bond!" Sinclair pleaded so desperately it embarrassed her husband.

"Today is Sunday. No court today but I'll get a hearing in a day or two. If, we get a bond, it won't be cheap," McCoy advised.

"I don't care! We'll pay it no matter what it is!" Mrs Rollins declared while Mr Rollins thought, 'sheeeeet' to himself.

"Speaking of fees," the lawyer slithered since the door to the vault was open. Friend or no friend he was going to tax the Rollins family. Once the news broke of the star athlete's murder this case would be huge. He may as well adjust his prices now. Especially if he could pull off his self defense angle.

"We'll pay it! Whatever it is!" she offered again like she earned some of the money. She didn't even fuck her husband enough to add to the bank accounts.

"What are we looking at?" Mr Rollins needed to know.

"Well, my fee will be one hundred thousand dollars. The bond, if we get one, would be at least another hundred, two hundred perhaps."

"Two hundred thousand dollars! I don't have two hundred thousand dollars!" he fussed.

"Sure we do! We have that in savings. We can mortgage the house if need be!" she insisted.

"I don't know about?" he questioned since he was the one who saved that money and paid for this house. Hearing anyone spend it so quickly without consultation was a shock. Especially to bring a cold blooded killer back under the same room.

"Don't know about what! Our son, is going to jail for something he didn't do!" Sinclair fussed. The two men shared a glance as to who would give her the news. Carey sighed since this was his home, his wife and his responsibility.

"He did it. There's video," he admitted. "Carey killed him."

"He did it, but it was self defense!" the lawyer proclaimed. "And, there's video to support it!"

The Rollins looked on as McCoy pulled up one of the many videos circulating around the web. He selected this one since it picks up just as Marquis picks Carey junior up and slams him on his head. Both parents winced when they watched their son get knocked out cold.

"This victim is no victim at all! He's from the ghetto! Been arrested for an act of violence. Ran with criminal street gangs!" McCoy happily laid out. It was a stretch but he planned to spin it like Charlotte's web.

"We still may need to talk to a few more lawyers, get a second opinion..." Carey offered.

"Pay the man you spineless bastard! Get my son out of jail!" she demanded and pounded on his chest. McCoy saw the bumps and lumps on the woman and didn't know if his old friend had given them to her or not. If he did, more might be coming from her attack.

"I have a few stops to make. Just call me when you make a decision," the lawyer said and excused himself. Mrs Rollins was out the door right after him and cornered him at his car.

"I need you to help my son! We'll pay you! I'll do anything!" she vowed.

"Anything can be a lot," he smirked and looked back towards the house. His friend went to fix a drink and wasn't looking outside.

"I meant what I said..." she said and gripped his dick through his slacks. She didn't bother to check to see if her husband was checking for her because she just didn't care. All that matters was getting her son out of jail.

"I'm going to take you up on your offer," he said and got hard in her hand. "I'ma need my bread first tho!"

"This nasty ass hoe!" Marquita growled as she watched the spectacle from her window. She could clearly see Carey's car was in the driveway which meant he was home while his wife gripped the next dick in the driveway. The anger took her mind off the grim task at hand since she had to now claim her son's remains and arrange his burial.

CHAPTER 16

"Is Carey here?" McCoy asked as he entered the Rollins home. Purely rhetorical since Carey senior's car wasn't in the driveway. Carey junior's car hadn't moved since the night of the murder. He had been booked into the jail but they managed to have him held in medical but only for a few days.

"Of course not. That's why I told you to come over," she said and went straight for his zipper. The lawyer took a Superman pose as she pulled his dick out. Only because getting head kinda makes you feel like Superman.

"I, need, my, son, 'gawk', out of, 'gawk', jail..." she said and sucked at the same time.

"I need, mmmm, my money," he said because if she thought some head would make up for his fee she was crazy. He had worked for free thus far but they needed to straighten him out before he went to court.

Men are more pliable after a good nut so she threw her head and neck into overdrive. The technique was lacking due to lack of practice but a blow job is a blow job and she ultimately got the job done.

"Argh!" Mrs Rollins reeled, gagged and spit when she ended up with a mouthful of salty semen. McCoy shook his head since women like this still confused him. What exactly did she expect would happen after sucking and tugging on a dick.

"Carey's a lucky man!" he gasped and gushed as he tucked his still erect dick away. Rule number one in fucking a married woman in her own home is put your dick away as soon as possible. If Carey had come in just then they could make excuses. Ain't no excuses with your dick out.

Rule number two is ain't no going to sleep over there. It matters not how good the head or tail is, don't go to sleep at a chick's house. Trouble just did it and some hating ass nigga killed him over a chick who didn't want him.

"He is!" she cosigned. She was so delusional she still thought she was doing her husband a favor by being his wife. She proved she was a good mother by taking one to the tonsils for her child.

"Look, get him to put the house up for bail. That way he's not spending cash, because I need mine in cash," the lawyer said and walked towards the door.

"You'll have a check today!" she assured him as she walked him to the car. There was an awkward moment when she and Marquita locked eyes from across the street.

"Don't say anything to her! The worst thing you can do is engage the mother. You're the victim, remember that," he coached and got into his car.

"Hmp!" Sinclair huffed and lifted her chin before heading back into the house herself. Right inside to forge her husband's name on the forms to pull one hundred thousand dollars from their retirement accounts.

CAREY WATCHED and waited in the window but saw no signs of Marquita. It made sense that she wasn't in the mood to wash her car the day before her son's funeral. Luckily the school boosters stepped up and paid for all expenses so she didn't have to set up a funding campaign to bury her son.

"Fuck it..." he decided and marched downstairs and out of the house. He was livid that his wife practically stole their retirement funds to pay the lawyer. Then had the audacity to take an extra fifty thousand dollars out for any incidentals Duane said could arise. If that wasn't bad enough she signed his name again to use the house as collateral to bail him out of jail. The judge set bond at the half million dollar value of the family home. She was at the jail waiting for his ankle monitors so she could bring him home so Carey desperately needed someone to talk to.

The story his wife gave didn't add up so he reviewed the Ring can footage. He clearly saw the lawyer visit no one told him about and it made sense. He felt like the odd man out in his own home, and that's not a good feeling.

"Huh?" Marquita asked in utter confusion when she opened the door and saw him standing there.

"I um, just, I..." he stammered, suddenly unsure of why he was there. One thing did come to mind so he offered that. "I'm sorry. I'm just so sorry for what my son did."

Marquita tilted her head when the man broke down in heavy sobs. She had moped around for days with no one to console her but now found herself consoling the father of the man who killed her baby.

"I'm sorry he did too," she said and wrapped him up. They both found comfort in the embrace and held on. Marquita tasted the salt from her tears in her open mouth. It wasn't until they pulled away that she noticed they were his tears.

"She went to get him," he revealed. It dawned on him that he had trouble saying his name even though it was his own name. "They gave him a bail."

"I figured. Y'all rich folk do what y'all wanna do," she huffed.

"That's not..." he began to protest but realized it was true. To make matters worse the defense planned to make the victim out to be the bad guy. He didn't have it in him to tell her about that part. Nor did he agree with it, but was powerless to do anything. He's not sure how he went from head of household to a do-boy, sugar daddy.

"Mmhm," she hummed and twisted her lips as she took a seat on the sofa. She needed the company but couldn't ask him to stay. She missed their weekly talks but still, wouldn't ask him to stay. She wouldn't need to since he plopped down beside her.

"Honestly, I don't even want to be there. With either of them," he admitted to even his own surprise. That turned her head but she didn't have a response.

"Hmp, makes sense," she nodded after a moments silence,

"What does?" he asked after his own moment of silence couldn't make it out.

"I had an uncle who went to prison for a long time. My mama's brother. He came home when I was about fifteen?" she asked, nodded and continued. "He used to stand in the window and watch and my lil friends jump rope and play hopscotch. I used to wonder what he was doing so one day I snuck in the back 'doe. Came around and caught him going at it!"

"Going at what?" he chuckled with her contagious laughter. She made a motion with her hand like a man jerking off and peered knowingly into his soul. Only his brownness saved him from blushing. "Oh!"

"Mmhm. I be seeing you watching me. I was hoping you was jacking while watching me. That's why I always waited til yo nasty ass wife left. Then, be bending and squatting 'fo you," she admitted and tilted her head to see how he was taking it. "I hope you got yo self a good one?"

"I, I um, I..." Carey stammered uncomfortably before giving up. "It's the only sex I had in months!"

126

"But did you get a good one? A good nut?" she wanted to hear.

"Like the world was ending!" he admitted and laughed. Sometimes a good laugh can help get past the pain.

The friends shared a good laugh but it didn't last long. The laughter died in their throats when they heard his wife pull into the driveway. She and

Carey junior bounded into happily into the house to go on liv

ing while she had to deal with the death. Carey didn't budge since he didn't want to see either of them. No telling how long he would have stayed if she hadn't made him go.

"You better go," she advised and stood. Carey watched her round ass shift down the hall and into her room before he got up. Marquita pulled her phone and made the call she had contemplated for days.

"Sup 'Quita," the same uncle who used to jack off while watching her and her friends play asked when he took the call.

"Hey, unc? I need a gun..."

The End, for now

EPILOGUE

"$\mathcal{H}$mm?" Latisha hummed when she came across another ghost gun in the internal police blotter. The metropolitan Atlanta area was made up of many different jurisdictions. The fluid borders made it easy for criminals to spread their dirt around town. The cops got smart and started the database to share information.

"What you got?" her partner asked in between stalking Mrs Worthington. He couldn't seem to get her back on the line after the night they spent in the hotel.

He knew he laid the pipe like a whole pro so it didn't register that she was ducking him. He got a lot of ass after funerals and shootings, when women were vulnerable, but none like this. She was clean and fresh and came every few minutes.

"Another one. Looks just like ours..." she said and scooted away from the screen when he came over for a look. He had a bad habit of leaning the dick on her back when he looked over her shoulder. They may have shared a few ill gotten gains but there would be no sharing of body fluids.

"Looks just like ours!" he announced and looked at the name on the file. "Carey Rollins. Where do I know that name from?"

"From the Worthington boy. Killed at the gas station. They were best friends and sold drugs together according to the sister," Latisha recalled. "Wouldn't it be crazy if it's connected to our unsolved case?"

"Ole Man-man?" Johnson scrunched his face and tilted his head. The shell casings came from a ghost gun but that was a stretch. Or was it?

Guess we'll find out in vol. 2

THE CHAMP

THE CHRONICLES OF A JUNKY...

By

Sa'id Salaam

PROLOGUE

"Willie?" my mom asked from room to room in the sing song tone reserved for me, her precious, precarious three year old.

"Are you hiding from me?" she asked as her search yielded no results. "Boy where are you?"

My mother's tone went from playful to frustrated to concern when she spied the sliding glass patio door was open. Panic set in as her eyes quickly shot to the open fence that surrounded our in-ground pool.

"Willieeee!" she screamed for both me and my dad who graciously allowed me to share his name.

When my mother came into view, I was looking up from the bottom of the pool. She screamed frantically for me but my lungs were full of water so I couldn't reply.

That's when it happened. I actually left my body and began rising out of the pool. My dad passed me on the way down to retrieve my body.

I watched peacefully as I rose higher above the scene. As my dad brought me to the surface, my mom pulled my body from my father allowing him to climb from the pool.

"Call 911," he yelled, sending mom flying back to the house. I watched as my dad began chest compressions that forced the water from my lungs. Every time he pressed I seemed to descend. Finally, with one last thrust I was back in my body coughing furiously.

"Thank God!" my father exclaimed, as he pulled me into his arms. My mother, who just returned, echoed his sentiment exactly.

Even though my parents spoke of that day from time to time during my life, I did not remember it—until now—now that I'm rising above my body again.

CHAPTER 1

*M*y name is William Champion and I am a junky. I don't particularly like that label but I do like to get high, so it is what it is. I know the term usually elicits a dirty, run-down addict nodding on a street corner. However, I am, or at least was, the polar opposite.

I was raised in the upscale Atlanta suburb Dunwoody. My neighborhood boasted homes starting at half a mil. Most of the residents were old money. Most households had a Mercedes outside in the driveway and both parents inside.

We were no exception. My dad William Champion, Sr. grew up there attending the superior schools and connecting with future movers and shakers like himself.

After graduating from the prestigious Dunwoody Prep, he attended Atlanta Tech and excelled in its engineering department.

My father was tall and possessed the solid frame of an athlete, but never played sports. Nonetheless, he did catch the eye of a pretty co-ed I now call Mom.

My mother was from the hood. She grew up in the rough streets of Decatur, Georgia, a quaint suburb, next door to

Atlanta, with an incredible murder rate. The eldest of two children, my mother's main goal was getting out of the hood. At 18 she moved into the dorms of Atlanta Tech on a full scholarship never to return...ever.

That meant leaving her younger sister, who already showed a penchant for the streets, to the streets. It was her chance and she took it.

As a result, six years later at 15, my aunt Betty gave birth to my cousin Brett, a week after I was born. Brett and I didn't get to spend a lot of time together as kids but were close nonetheless.

At times when my mom was bickering or lecturing her sister, Brett could spend nights at our house but, I was never allowed to sleep over their house.

By high school, both Brett and I were star athletes each excelling in our chosen sports.

He was hands down the best wide receiver in the state, if not the country. Me, I was the best point guard on the east coast. Although there is the possibility I could go pro, the focus was my education.

While some kids loathe to follow in a parent's footsteps, that's all I aspired to do. I intend to go to Atlanta Tech and excel at engineering, just like my dad.

Like my dad, I had my future wife secured already. Prentice and I had been groomed to be together since kindergarten. Our parents were close and arranged our marriage early. I assumed they considered their combined stock would produce healthy, good looking, high IQ grandbabies.

Prentice was prim, proper and very sadity. Her long brown hair was augmented with streaks of blonde that perfectly framed her pretty face. She, of course, is a virgin which makes me one too.

Being a star athlete, I get hit on a lot but I'm dating the head cheerleader so I decline all offers. Even if it means settling for the occasional hand job I can beg her out of every once in a while.

My cousin Brett on the other hand has fucked half the girls in Decatur. He sent pictures to my e-mail of all kinds of girls doing all kinds of stuff. Sometimes I have to give myself a hand job after looking at all that.

Since our parents couldn't come together and organize a graduation cookout, we had them back to back.

Mine of course was a catered affair, complete with tents and fountains set up in our back yard. Everyone chatted in quiet little groups, while the live band played soft rock hits from the 80's.

Everyone was properly dressed – men in chinos and polos, women in long flowing sundresses.

"Say Shawty, dat fuck nigga tried to card me to get a drank!" Brett fumed when he returned from the bar.

"All they have is white wine anyway," I offered as consolation.

"Good thang I brought my loud pack," he said, producing a nearly rolled blunt.

"Dude, my mom would absolutely lose her mind if you lit that," I said near panic.

"Chill Shawty," Brett laughed, "I see it ain't that type of party. Come thru tomorrow and we finna do it up."

"Roger that," I agreed as hiply as I could. Guess not hip enough because my cousin laughed as he went to his car.

CHAPTER 2

"*S*essalie, that boy is 18 years old," I heard my father say in my defense, "just graduated and has been away for weeks at a time. What's the big deal about spending a night at your sister's house?"

"First," my mom began, in her attempt to forbid me from sleeping over after Brett's cookout, "my sister is ghetto. She will not supervise the kids."

"OK and so what? They'll have fun?" My dad chuckled.

"You don't understand that neighborhood, those people," my mom sighed.

"Those people? Black people? Your sister?" my dad asked before putting his foot down. "Tell him *WE* said it's fine."

"OK," mom said, ever the obedient wife, "but mark my words, he'll never be the same."

"Yessss!!!" I said, pumping a fist as I eavesdropped.

I hurried down the hall and ducked into my room before my mother came out. After a laundry list of do's and don'ts she shared what I already knew. I could spend the night in 'da hood'.

Bret's BBQ was held in an alternative universe than the one I hosted the day before. Dudes all had on baggy shorts pulled down to expose their boxers and over half were shirtless; and the girls…oh…my…God! They were naked. Cleavage and ass cheeks everywhere. I made an appointment with myself for a hand job as soon as the party was over. If I made it that long.

There were no caterers fussing about, just Brett on the grill, and beer runs. Feeling a little, well a lot out of my element I stuck close to Brett and took it all in.

"Hey baby," a tall Tyra Banks looking stallion sang and gave my cousin a juicy kiss.

"What's good shawty," Brett drawled as soon as her tongue cleared his mouth. "Dis my cuzn Willie, Willie dis my gal Tonya."

"Pleased to meet you Tonya," I said, extending my hand.

"Hey Willie," Tonya managed between chuckles, "dis my gurl Mel."

I turned to speak to her friend but got stuck. Standing before me was a chocolate colored girl who made time stop. She wore a mesh dress that left nothing to the imagination. My dick got so hard, so quick, I nearly fainted.

"You aight cuzn?" Brett asked as my knees buckled.

After I got myself together, the four of us kicked it. I politely declined all offers of weed and alcohol. Mel flirted non-stop the whole time.

It was near midnight when the inevitable fight broke out. After all the liquor, weed, and chicken, all that was left was a fight.

Two guys went at it pretty good while their cliques looked on. I was scared to death, but my cousin never even looked up from the grill.

Once the gladiators finished beating on each other, the party resumed, as if the fracas never happened.

"Shawty digging you cuz," Brett announced as he took the last of the meat off the grill.

"Who?" I asked, even though I should have known better.

Mel had been staring at me since she arrived.

I realized hood chicks are far more aggressive than the girls in my universe. She been licking her lips and blowing me kisses all night.

"Who you think nigga?" My cousin chuckled, "She done set the ass out for you. All you gotta do is take it."

"Cuzo you know I'm in a committed relationship with Prentice," I replied, sounding corny even to myself.

"Nigga, you in the presence of a stone cold freak and you talking shit about a chick who won't even let you touch the pussy," Brett said, walking into the house.

I again surveyed my surroundings with amazement. These kids were my age and younger but everyone, everyone was both smoking weed and drinking.

I'm not sure what propelled me to the cooler but there I went. I extracted an ice cold beer and opened it. My first sip of beer caused me to frown from the bitterness. The second was a gulp and the next finished the green bottle.

Eager to catch up with everyone else, I pulled another one out the ice and cracked it.

"Not you cuz," Brett laughed, returning from inside.

"I guess you was right, it ain't gone kill me," I replied, showing off the ebonics I'd just learned.

"Say yall," Bret announced loudly, "party ova! You ain't gotta go home but you gotta get the fuck outa here!"

It took a few minutes for the crowd to exit the backyard. When the last person left, Brett, Tonya, Mel and myself settled into the den.

"I'm finna put in a movie," Mel said, bending over to make a selection. When she bent over, her ass strained against the mesh giving a clear shot of how well developed she was.

"You aight ova dere cuzn?" Bret laughed, seeing my reaction.

"Yeah I'm cool," I replied, glad they couldn't see the real reaction straining my pants to be set free.

"Smoke one?" Tonya asked, huddling up close to Brett.

"Shit, I been on dat grill all day. Yall do it," he said, tossing a bag of weed on the table.

It looked more like green popcorn to me as I inspected it. The girls looked at me as if I was expected to roll the blunt but I wouldn't know where to begin.

"I got it," Mel announced, grabbing the weed off the table.

I got another erection when she slid her tongue around the cigar to moisten it. I watched in fascination as she split the cigar with a pinky nail, then dumped the guts on the table.

She crumbled up a good amount of the fluffy weed and tucked it inside. When she re-rolled it using her saliva to seal it, I made up my mind to try it. I wanted to be anywhere her tongue had been.

I was already feeling the mellow effects of my first beer when I took my first pull off my first blunt. By the time a full rotation had been completed, I was good and high and I loved it!

Tonya and Brett were making out pretty good, so it was no surprise when they got up and rushed from the room.

"So what's up?" Mel said, seductively sliding closer.

"With what?" I stammered.

"I'm saying," she replied and kissed me. It was the first time I'd kissed anyone other than Prentice or my mom, and neither of them used their tongue. Mel ran her hands over my body as we kissed, until stumbling upon the wood.

"Damn Boy!" she exclaimed because of how hard I was.

It felt so good to be out of the confines of my pants when she pulled my dick out, but then she worked her hand better than Prentice or I ever did.

She pulled my shirt off and sucked my nipples and chest, as I fought not to cum. I recalled the last hand job Prentice gave me months back, and how she flipped when a little cum got on her hand.

I then experienced a sensation like I could never have dreamed. *Nah, it can't be,* I said to myself before looking down. When I did, I saw Mel had half of my dick in her mouth and I exploded.

"Mmm," Mel moaned, milking my dick with her hand. At that moment, I decided to skip school, leave Prentice, run away and just stay right here…inside her mouth.

Mel went and got us another beer. When she came back in the den, she slipped her dress off, slid her thong to the side and straddled me. As much as I wanted to fuck her, my body wasn't ready yet. We shared the beer, as we licked and sucked on each other's naked bodies.

She smiled when she felt me rise again. She lined me up with her vagina and wriggled me inside. A condom crossed my mind but the weed and alcohol said it would be OK without one. She slid slowly down my rock hard dick and by the time she reached the bottom, I came again!

"Dang boy," Mel chuckled, "I know I got some good pussy but let me get a nut too!"

"I'm sorry" was all I could think of to say in my moment of satisfaction.

We took a break to smoke another blunt, then went at it some more. She showed me positions I didn't think possible. I calmed down enough for her to begin riding me. Although the effects of the beer and her riding me had me feeling a little weird, I didn't want it to end. This time I managed to control my excitement for about 10 minutes and then she made us both cum. Mel sexed me for the rest of the night.

Looking back on that night of many firsts I'd have to say, that's what turned me out…Did me in. Too many pleasures at once.

Over the course of the summer I was so busy with basketball camps and orientation that I didn't indulge in anymore sex or drugs, but I thought about them both everyday.

CHAPTER 3

*S*ince Brett had a scholarship to Atlanta Tech as well, my dad let us use his condo downtown. While most kids dealt with musty dorms, we had it made.

The condo was an investment property my dad purchased years back and had quadrupled in value since. We were living in luxury.

I began smoking weed again, every chance I got. I saw Mel every chance I got. She and Tonya would come spend the night a couple times a week. Brett had a few more girls but I was content with Mel.

My cousin had been selling weed all summer and kept the best weed in the house. Everyday it's kush, or dro, or purp.

I was living a double life. There was William, the star athlete/honor student, and cool Will who drank and smoked a little. I enjoyed being Will more and more by the day.

Brett's weed business was obviously doing well, based on the new Lexus he came home with. It was the same model as mine. Only differences was the color and source of income to pay for it. Mine was a graduation present from my parents. The streets paid for his.

We started hitting the strip clubs pretty regularly and got carte blanche everywhere we went. I tried my best to be faithful to Prentice's hand but my cousin brings home two or three, sometimes four women every night.

One night, we brought a couple of strippers home from the club. Destiny and Unique proved there is a God. They were perfect! Perfect face, teeth, eyes, breasts, ass...just perfect.

As soon as Brett spotted them he offered to pay them for the night, if they left with us. I couldn't hear the negotiations but we all left together.

I had since learned to roll a decent blunt and did so while Brett went to his room. He came back a few minutes later and handed Unique a plastic bag of white powder.

"Heeeyyy! That's what I'm talking about!" she exclaimed happily.

Let's get this party started!" Destiny announced.

I watched in awe as the two perfect women made perfect little lines on the glass table. Destiny rolled a dollar bill and snorted two long lines up her perfect nose.

"What's that?" I asked anxiously as she fell back in ecstasy.

"Don't tell me you ain't never seen no powder honey!" Unique chuckled before mimicking Destiny.

"You studying that shit kinda hard," Brett said harshly, noticing my gaze never left the pile of cocaine on the table.

"Huh? Oh naw I'm cool," I replied, even though I still hadn't looked away from the drugs on the table.

I inhaled deeply on the blunt, secretly wishing I could try the shiny white powder

The girls snorted, drank and smoked until all stimulants had been exhausted.

Well let's get to it!" Brett announced with a hand clap.

"Y'all want us to dance?" Destiny asked, as she rubbed her nose.

"Naw I'm tryna fuck something," he replied, grabbing Unique's hand.

"That's what's up! This blow got me horny," she replied as he led her from the room.

"Well?" Destiny asked as soon as were alone. I took the hint and led her to my bedroom.

"Nice!" she exclaimed at the luxury I took for granted.

As she entered, she began to undress. By the time she reached her bra and panties, I was in my boxers.

"Damn!" Destiny laughed, grabbing my rock hard dick. "You betta not cum all quick. I'm tryna get mines too!"

"OK," was all I could think to say.

"Here," she said, digging into her purse. "Take a bump. It'll make that thang stay hard."

I complied willingly. She lifted a pinky nail loaded with coke. I inhaled the two scoops she offered and felt its effects instantly.

My mind, body and soul went numb. Destiny was right, I stayed hard all night and punished her. The cocaine coursing through my system made me feel like Superman.

The next morning after we dropped the girls off, Brett and I stopped for breakfast. We ordered our food and waited silently for it to arrive.

"Say cuz, what was that about last night?" I finally asked.

"Yeah, I was trippin Shawty," he offered by way of an apology. "I just don't really like them coke hoes. Can't trust 'em."

"I feel you," I said, not feeling him at all. Destiny was cool and the sex was ridiculous! "That girl got some fire head… almost as good as Mel!"

"One I had too! Suck the skin off a dick," Brett laughed. "Speaking of Mel I heard she on the blow too. That's why Tonya don't fuck with her no more."

That explained why I hadn't seen or heard from Mel lately,

even though Tonya frequents the apartment. We went on to fill each other in on the night's freaky festivities. I chose not to talk about the

Made in the USA
Columbia, SC
23 August 2022

65267384R00085